Cooper's Last Resort

KIRT J BOYD

Cooper's Last Resort

 This is a work of fiction. Names, characters, businesses, places, events and incidents are either the products of the author's imagination or used in a fictitious manner. Any resemblance to actual persons, living or dead, or actual events is purely coincidental.

Printed in the United States of America

ISBN 978-0-09883153-5-8

Rolling Down the Mountain Press

Cover Design by Donna Harriman
DHMDesigns.net
Kitikat4u.deviantART.com
DHMDesigns.99designs.com

FOR MY FAMILY

ALSO BY KIRT J BOYD

The Last Stop

Grandma vs. the Tornado and Other Stories

Chapter One

Stanley was running late. There were few things that flustered him this late in life, but not being on time was one of them, even if all he was late for was breakfast with his friend Ned from down the hall. Ned wasn't likely to care much one way or the other. He'd probably just order his coffee like usual and read the paper until Stanley arrived, but Stanley liked routine. Ned always told him that he ran his life like a Navy ship, which was both true and ironic considering Stanley had been in the Navy but hadn't liked it much.

His morning was supposed to start at six o'clock on the nose, when his Swiss Army wristwatch alarm went off, but sometime during the night his watch battery had died, leaving him lying awake in bed wondering what time it was based on the angle of the sun streaming in through his window. His watch said three forty-five, which wasn't much help. He was pretty certain it wasn't three forty-five in the afternoon. He knew it was later than six o'clock, though, by the way his stomach was growling. He had eaten breakfast at the same time for as long as he could remember and his stomach was reminding him of the fact.

He didn't have a clock in his room. His fancy Swiss Army wristwatch had met all of his clock and calendar requirements. Now that it was essentially an elaborate, nonfunctional bracelet, he made a mental note to invest in some sort of backup.

He rolled over and out of bed and hustled out into the kitchen to check the clock on the microwave. Seven-fifteen. He knew it was a little fast, but he couldn't remember by how much. It had been a long time since he'd paid any attention to it. Either way, he decided that it wasn't late enough to go out looking like he'd just fallen out of bed, so he hurried into the bathroom, brushed his teeth, shaved and showered. He knew this was something Ned would later give him a hard time about. There weren't many people who cared what he looked like these days. He could have just as easily ran a comb through his hair and been done with it, but he knew he would be uncomfortable. Maybe no one else cared what he looked like, but he did. Besides, there was a chance that his lady friend, Lillian, would show up, so he wanted to look nice.

He put on his pressed slacks and blue golf shirt, and then slipped on his New Balance tennis shoes. Then he returned to the bathroom and used the hair gel Frank the barber had given him and slicked his hair straight back, leaving just enough spring to make things interesting. Once he was satisfied with how he looked, he wiped down the counter and mirror and shut off the light. Exiting his room, he hurried down the Aspen wing and into the restaurant where he found Ned in their usual booth in the corner, looking at him over the top of his newspaper.

"Don't look at me like that," Stanley said. "Go back to your paper. Did you order already?"

"Well, yeah," Ned said. "You want me to sit here and starve to death? I ordered your coffee, but I drank it. I ordered another one, but Tracey hasn't brought it yet."

"Thanks."

"I'd say you look terrible, but that wouldn't be accurate. You look spiffy as always, but you seem out of sorts. Late night last night?"

"Late morning, more like it. My watch battery died."

Ned looked at the Swiss Army watch on Stanley's wrist.

"Yet you still wear it . . ."

"I like the way it looks."

"Anyway," Ned said. "That's why I have an alarm clock by my bed."

"I don't like alarm clocks. I don't like getting jarred awake. This," Stanley said, tapping the face of his watch, "brings me gently out of sleep."

"Right," Ned said. "Until this morning. My question is this: Why in the world do we even have alarms? Look around you, we're retired! What would happen, I mean really, if we slept until noon?"

"I'd be so hungry I couldn't get out of bed. I haven't missed breakfast in twenty years."

"And we both know how you get when you're hungry."

"Exactly."

Tracey appeared holding a tray of food.

"Just in time!" Ned said. "Stanley's head was about to start spinning around. I ordered for you. Two sausage links, two eggs over—"

"Sorry," Tracey said, "but I had to give you bacon. The new kid left the sausage on the counter last night, so Amato had to throw it out."

"That's fine," Stanley said.

"You don't happen to have a watch battery, do you?" Ned asked. "That would really cheer him up."

"Okay . . ." Tracey said, and walked off.

Stanley started on his breakfast, wrapping one of the pieces of bacon in a slice of toast. Ned started on his blueberry pancakes.

"I get that you were late getting up," Ned said. "And I

get that you were hungry, but you're eating now and you apparently got more sleep than you're used to, so you'd think you'd be all perky and glowing, yet the crease in your forehead only grows. You and Lillian okay?"

Stanley couldn't help but detect the hopeful note in Ned's voice that everything was not all right, so he looked out the window without answering. Harry, the maintenance man, and Holy Moses, the facility's hundred and forty-eight pound canine mascot, were trying to play a game of fetch. The only problem was that Harry wanted Holy to fetch it, and Holy wanted Harry to fetch it, leaving them in a strange sort of standoff.

"Sorry, what were you saying?" Stanley said.

"I was asking you about Lillian."

"Oh, we're fine. My grandkid is coming to stay for the summer—you're about to dribble syrup on your shirt."

"Excuse me?"

"Your shirt—"

"No, no, before that."

"My grandkid is coming to stay with me for the summer."

"Can he do that? I mean, they'll let him just come and stay?"

"They will if he volunteers. I thought I told you all of this. They've got him lined up to help out here at the restaurant. He's having all sorts of problems at school. His mother is already worried he's not going to graduate and he just started high school. She thinks it would be good for him."

"How old is he?"

"Fifteen."

"She thinks it would be good for a fifteen-year-old kid to come live at a retirement home?"

"No, she thinks it would be good for him to spend the summer with his grandfather, who just happens to live in a retirement home. Besides, she thinks it would be good for him to work."

"She obviously doesn't know Amato," Ned said. "So, what's the matter? You don't want him to come?"

"I'm seventy-seven years old. I'm set in my ways. I don't know that I'm up for straightening out a fifteen-year-old kid, whom I haven't even seen in three years. What are we going to do when he's not working? He's used to California. What do I know about California? And according to his mother, he's moody."

"California, huh? Rough. What does he like to do?"

"I don't know. He probably wants to be in a band or something," Stanley said. "His mom wasn't much help. It doesn't sound like they're getting along very well these days."

Ned scooted his empty plate to the edge of the table and said, "Probably on drugs. You better search him when he gets here, that's all I'm saying. You don't want some California kid selling drugs out of your room."

"Selling them to whom, exactly?" Stanley asked.

Ned came around to Stanley's side of the booth and whispered, "Hathaway's been awfully giddy lately."

"Hathaway? The Hustler Hathaway? The woman who spends all of her free time beating everyone at poker and thirty-one? The woman who rides around in a perfectly unnecessary wheelchair so everyone will think she's frail?"

"I saw her the other day sitting by herself outside on the swing, laughing for no reason."

"You laugh for no reason all the time," Stanley reminded him. "It's probably just part of the act. Now that everyone thinks she's frail, she wants them to think she's lost her marbles, too."

"Marijuana is legal now, you know?" Ned said. "Check him, that's all I'm saying."

"Check him for what?" Lillian said. Neither one of them had seen her coming. Ned returned to his side of the booth, and Lillian slid in next to Stanley, snatching a piece of bacon off his plate.

"His grandson is a drug-head," Ned said.

"He's not a drug-head. He's a confused fifteen-year-old. He's probably hanging around the wrong crowd. It doesn't mean he's on drugs."

"I bet he's a good kid," Lillian said. "Most of them are if you stop treating them like kids. That's what brings out their bad side."

"See, the voice of reason," Stanley said and kissed her hand.

"Stop it," Lillian said. "You're going to give me the coots."

Stanley laughed. Ned said, "You look particularly pretty today, Lillian."

Ned was always complimenting Lillian in front of Stanley because he knew it got on his nerves, but the truth was that Stanley didn't know quite how to define his relationship with Lillian. What did you call a woman who you went to dinner with a few times a week and who occasionally stayed over? At their age, calling her his girlfriend seemed silly.

"Oh, Ned," Lillian said, grabbing his hand and squeezing it. "You're so sweet. If only you weren't so short . . ."

Stanley laughed. She was always getting on Ned about his height, which at five-foot-six-inches wasn't really that short.

"I don't know why you're laughing," Lillian told Stanley. "At least he pays me compliments."

"I tell you you're beautiful all the time," Stanley said. "It's not my fault if you don't believe me."

"Short, she says," Ned said, looking exasperated. "Look around you, lady! Out there," he said, pointing out the window, "I'm short. In here, I'm perfectly average."

"If you say so," Lillian said. Turning to Stanley, she said, "So when does the little bundle of joy get here and when do I get to meet him?"

"Wait," Ned said, looking from Lillian to Stanley and back again. "You knew about this?"

They both ignored him. Stanley said, "He's coming in this afternoon. I figure I'll let him get settled tonight before I bombard him with all you people."

"You tell her, but you don't tell your best friend?" Ned said.

"I thought I told you. Calm down."

"Well, now you've done it," Lillian said. "You've gone and hurt little Ned's feelings. He told me, Ned, because we talk about things like that. You two talk about sports and the weather and horse racing and who knows what. We talk about other stuff. That's what you do when you're sleeping together."

"Oh, geez," Ned said.

Lillian laughed. "Good lord," she said. "Look at you two, blushing like a couple of school kids!"

Tracey stopped by the table to see if Lillian wanted something to eat.

"No," Lillian said. "Just stopped by to see what the old guys were up to. A cup of coffee would be great. I'm feeling a bit oogy this morning."

Oogy was code for hungover. Lillian didn't drink often, but when she did, she did it right.

"Tied one on, did you?" Ned asked. "Surprised I didn't hear you from down the hall and around the corner."

Lillian rolled her eyes and sipped her coffee. She might be mad about what Ned said, but she couldn't refute it. The truth was that she tended to be loud regardless of the situation. When she drank, she tended to come across with all the subtlety of a runaway freight train.

"So, what's his name?" Ned asked when it was obvious that Lillian wasn't going to give him anything to work with.

"Cooper," Stanley said.

"Cooper . . . Cooper . . . Cooper. Nope, don't think I

know any Coopers," Ned said.

"Would it have mattered if you did?" Stanley asked.

"I think it's a good name," Lillian said. "Sounds a bit mischievous, though. Is he a pothead, do you think?"

"What is it with you people? Every troubled teen isn't a pothead," Stanley said.

"But he's from California," Ned said, "and you know how they run out there."

"No, Ned, I don't know. Tell me, how do they run?"

"Fast. That's all I'm saying. Fast and loose and high and dry."

Lillian laughed. Stanley shook his head.

"Laugh if you want," Ned said, "but when you smell the ganja, don't come running to me."

"Ms. Hathaway smokes," Lillian said.

Ned banged his fist on the table. "I told you!"

"She says it's for some medical condition, but she's been laughing a lot lately."

Again Ned banged his fist on the table. "I told you!"

"So what's your plan?" Lillian asked.

"Plan?"

"You must have a plan. You can't just turn a fifteen-year-old boy loose around here, especially a troublemaker. He'll get mauled. You know how it is around here: youth is just an unfortunate stage to becoming an old person. What does he like to do?"

"I don't know. He rides his skateboard, I guess," Stanley said. "His mother thinks he might want to be in a band."

"See," Ned said, raising his eyebrows in Lillian's direction. "Drugs."

"What instrument does he play?" Lillian asked, ignoring Ned.

"I don't have any idea. I don't even know if it's true. She just kind of threw it out there."

Tracey showed up with Lillian's coffee. "These two aren't giving you any trouble, are they, Lillian?" This was an inside joke. They both knew that Stanley and Ned posed her no real threat, even if they ganged up on her. Lillian reached into her purse and handed Tracey a dollar.

"What's this?" Tracey asked.

"A tip. You made me laugh. You earned it."

"Hey Tracey," Ned said. "Ask Stanley what time it is."

"Very funny," Stanley said.

"I already know what time it is, Ned," Tracey said and left.

Lillian took a sip of coffee and snatched Stanley's last piece of bacon and ate it before he had time to complain. "Jesus, you eat like a bird," she said.

The intercom squeaked, and after a moment of feedback, Beverly, the receptionist, said, "Stanley Martin, please come to the main lobby. You have visitors."

Stanley looked at his watch.

"Still broken?" Ned asked.

"Jesus, they're early," Stanley said. "What time is it?"

"Twenty-five after eight," Ned said. "Maybe it's someone else."

"I don't know anyone else," Stanley said. "Everyone I know is in this building or dead."

Lillian scooted out of the booth so Stanley could get out. "Want me to go with you?" she asked.

"No," Stanley said. "I haven't told them about us."

"What is there to tell?" she asked.

Tracey saw them getting up to leave and came over with the bill. "You paying today, Ned?"

"Yes, he's paying," Stanley said.

"Is my coffee on there, too?" Lillian asked.

"These are my friends," Ned announced. "All they do is make fun of me and stick me with the bill. I am truly blessed! No, really, thank the good lord above that I've been blessed with friends such as these!"

"So, you're paying, then?" Tracey asked.

"Yes, I'm paying," Ned said.

"Here, you big baby," Stanley said, tossing a ten dollar bill on the table.

"Keep it," Ned said. "You'll need it to buy a new battery for your watch."

Chapter Two

Having not seen Cooper, not even in a picture, in over three years, Stanley didn't know quite what to expect. When he got to the lobby, he found a kid Cooper's age flicking the glass on the fish tank in the corner and he stopped in his tracks. From behind, the kid didn't look like the Cooper he remembered, but he knew very well the drastic changes that could take place once they entered their teenage years, boys especially. Unfortunately, the kid fit the description of everything Stanley didn't care for in today's youth. His hair hung in his eyes, for starters, and his pants hung too low. His left shoe was untied, and when Beverly asked him to kindly quit tapping on the glass because he was scaring the fish, he flashed a smirk that managed to seek out Stanley's spinal cord and made his left foot begin tapping involuntarily.

"I'm not scaring them," the kid said, and began banging on the glass with the palm of his hand.

Stanley had been thinking about how he was going to go about disciplining Cooper if the occasion arrived. He figured Cooper would test him at some point, he just didn't think it was going to happen within thirty seconds of their first meeting, if, indeed this was Cooper. Stanley approached the kid, figuring that the least he could do was distract him from the fish tank, when he heard from behind him, "Marcus! Quit banging on the glass. Get over here!" Stanley turned to find a woman, thankfully not his daughter, pointing her finger at the youth.

"I'm just looking," Marcus said.

"No, you're banging. Get away from the fish!"

"Whatever."

The woman turned to Stanley who was looking back and forth between them, smiling a little at the realization that this little monster wasn't Cooper. "That's his favorite word. You want a son?" Stanley put up his hands defensively. "No, no," he said.

"Hi, daddy." Stanley turned and found Melissa coming through the front doors. She looked tired. While she didn't talk about it to him much, he had gathered that her and Rick, her second husband, weren't doing so well. She had casually mentioned during their last phone conversation that Rick wasn't taking to the role of stepfather and it was putting a strain on their relationship. Cooper's real dad had been out of the picture except for the occasional birthday card since Cooper was three.

"Where's Coop?" Stanley asked, hugging her.

"He doesn't like to be called that anymore. He says it makes him sound like a child. He's getting his things out of the car."

Cooper's things amounted to a large duffel bag, a skateboard, and a cell phone. Stanley was happy to see the skateboard. It didn't seem like kids spent enough time outside these days.

While Cooper didn't have the permanent smirk of Marcus, there were still similarities. His hair, for instance, was much too long for Stanley's taste. One of the things he had gotten from his time in the military that had stuck was the love of a short, tight haircut. Cooper's hair hung in his eyes to the point where Stanley wondered how he could see where he was walking.

"Hi there, Coop . . . Er," Stanley said. "Need help carrying your stuff?" Stanley reached out to take his duffel bag, but Cooper stopped him.

"I'm fine," Cooper said.

" . . . Okay," Stanley said.

"Let him help you, Coop," Melissa said, and Stanley could tell by the way he looked at her that he indeed didn't like being called Coop. Now getting a good look at him, Stanley could understand why. He was still small for his age and he was still obviously self-conscience about it. It appeared he'd gotten slightly taller, but he had a lot of filling out to do. Cooper, he knew, had spent the majority of his life listening to people remarking about how small he was for his age, so Stanley thought he understood why he didn't like being called, Coop: It made him seem even younger than he looked. This was probably the same reason why Cooper didn't want Stanley helping him with his things.

Marcus had grown tired of the fish tank and wandered over to Cooper. "Let me see your board, kid," Marcus said, reaching for Cooper's skateboard. Marcus was probably the same age as Cooper, but he was a full head taller, and a whole lot heavier. Cooper didn't say anything, but he clutched his skateboard tighter to his side.

"Bet I'm better than you," Marcus said. When Cooper didn't answer, Marcus leaned down to where they were almost touching noses. "You deaf, kid? Come on. Let me see it!"

"Marcus!" His mother had finished talking to Beverly and stormed over to Marcus and grabbed him by his ear. "Sorry," she said. "Teenage boys. Let's go, Marcus." She let go of his ear, but shoved him out the door by the nape of his neck. Cooper hadn't so much as blinked during the whole altercation. Stanley had a feeling Cooper was used to this sort of thing. His size and quiet personality made him an easy target for kids like Marcus.

"Well," Melissa said. "You shouldn't have to deal with a lot of that here."

Stanley agreed. "Most of us are too old to pick on anyone," he said. Melissa laughed, but Cooper looked away.

"Okay, I have to go," Melissa said. "Come here and give me a hug and let me get out of here before I start crying."

"Moooom," Cooper said, drawing out the word, making it clear that she was embarrassing him.

"I'll call you in a few days and check on you. Oh, and daddy, make sure he's not playing on his phone all day. I swear it's like another appendage. And check his phone from time to time. I saw on 48 hours that girls his age send boys pictures of themselves with their tongues sticking out and stuff."

Stanley looked sideways at Cooper, trying to convey that he didn't have any intention of checking his phone. Of course, part of the reason for this was that he wouldn't have the first idea how to go about checking his phone, even if he wanted to.

"Anyway, have fun. Thank you, daddy," Melissa said, adding, "I just don't know what else to do." Stanley cringed at the fact that she said the last part in front of Cooper.

"Don't worry, we're going to have a great time," Stanley said, patting Cooper on the shoulder. "Right?"

"I guess so," Cooper said.

"He's a good kid. He just needs a change of scenery, that's all," Melissa said. She turned to Cooper. "Okay, try not to kill your grandfather," she said. She kissed them both on the forehead, ruffled Cooper's hair and left.

"Well, guess it's just me and you, kid," Stanley said. "You want some gum or something?"

Beverly, the receptionist, who had been quietly watching the whole interaction, said, "I've got some right here," and pulled a pack of Juicy Fruit out of her desk and held it out for him. Cooper walked over and took the gum and thanked her. "He gives you any trouble," she told him, motioning to Stanley, "you come find me. I'll straighten him out." She winked at him, and while it was hard to tell, Stanley thought he saw Cooper smile.

****

"Holy crow!" Cooper said. "He's huge!" They were back in Stanley's room. Stanley was preparing to give him the tour when Cooper spotted Holy Moses out the front-room window. Stanley had the good fortune of having a window that faced Holy's favorite bush with the purple flowers on it. During most spring and summer days, you could find Holy rolling around in front of this particular bush, snapping at the bumble bees. Stanley laughed at Cooper's reaction and joined him in front of the window. Watching people's reaction to seeing Holy Moses for the first time was one of the things Stanley enjoyed most.

"I bet you could ride him," Cooper said.

"You probably could, but I wouldn't recommend it," Stanley told him, chuckling a little. Over the years, a few kids had tried to saddle him and had been unceremoniously bucked off into the bushes.

"Is he mean?" Cooper asked.

"Not exactly. He won't bite you. He might make you feel bad about yourself, though."

Cooper turned to him with a puzzled look on his face, obviously trying to figure out how a dog could make you feel bad about yourself. But it was true. If Holy didn't want to spend time with you, it usually meant there was something in your life that needed tending to. Holy's similarities with the canine species ended with his physical form and his love of rolling around in freshly cut grass. In mannerisms and attitudes, he had much more in common with humans.

Holy apparently sensed that he was being watched

because he abruptly got up and wandered off.

"Okay," Stanley said, turning Cooper's attention to the couch. "This is where you'll sleep. It doesn't pull out or anything, but it's pretty comfortable." This may or may not have been true. Stanley had never actually slept on it, but it looked comfortable. If Stanley fell asleep anywhere but in his bed, it was almost always in his recliner.

Cooper's face revealed neither excitement nor displeasure at the thought of sleeping on a couch, though it was hard to tell for sure. Once Holy Moses was no longer a spectacle, Cooper's face went back to glum and disinterested. At least he thought it did. With his hair hanging in his face and his habit of always looking at the ground, it was hard to get a good read on him.

"How do you see anything with all that hair?" Stanley asked him, genuinely curious. To be fair, he knew that Cooper's hair was in line with other boys his age. He often saw them at the grocery store and on trips to the mall, especially, and he often wondered the same thing about them. Cooper didn't say anything, but Stanley heard him sigh. And though it was impossible to tell, he thought Cooper had probably rolled his eyes, too.

"If the couch is too uncomfortable, you can always sleep with your old granddad." He'd meant it as a joke, but the thought apparently alarmed Cooper because he looked up and quickly said, "No, it'll be okay."

On that note, Stanley continued the tour. As they went through the living quarters, Stanley was surprised by how small it really was. For one person, the small kitchen and dining area, the cozy living room and the one bedroom and bath was perfect, but now that there was going to be two of them sharing everything, it seemed impossibly small.

"There are more towels and things in the closet there, and the bathroom is around the corner. There's only the one, so if you have to drop a deuce—"

"A what?"

Lillian was fond of this particular expression in reference to taking a number two. It was funny and somehow fitting when she said it, but hearing himself say it out loud, he felt silly and old. If Lillian would have heard him say it, she'd have been on the floor rolling around with delight. Priceless, she would have said.

Stanley clarified: "If you have to go number two, give me a heads up and I'll do the same. It helps if you open the window in there, too, before you go." Stanley realized that this was a ridiculous conversation to be having, especially with a fifteen-year-old, but once the topic was brought up, he saw no choice but to see it through.

After taking a quick peek in the bedroom and the bathroom, Cooper settled on the couch and began playing with his phone.

"Nice phone you have there," Stanley said.

"It's the new IPhone," Cooper said without looking up. "It cost like $800."

Stanley's left leg gave out and it banged hard on the coffee table. "Your mother bought you an $800 phone?" he asked.

Cooper nodded.

"Pesos, you mean?"

"What?"

"Never mind. You want to see my phone?" Before Cooper had a chance to respond, Stanley disappeared into the bedroom and returned a minute later with the $29.99 pay-as-you-go phone he had bought during one of the community outings to the mall.

"Look," he said, "you flip it open like this. And you can talk to people on it, just like that deal there."

"Nobody has those anymore," Cooper said.

"That's not true," Stanley said. "I have one, and so does Ms. Fisher from down the hall."

"Okay," Cooper said, returning to his phone.

Stanley looked at his flip phone, shrugged and placed it

on the counter.

"I get up at six o'clock every morning," Stanley said, pausing a moment to wonder how that was going to go now that his watch was dead. "If you don't want to get up that early, I'll try to be quiet, but I can't make any guarantees," Stanley continued. "Most days you're going to be working the morning and afternoon shifts at the restaurant, so you're going to have to get used to getting up early anyway."

Cooper looked up. "Do I have to?"

"Not until Monday."

"Work, I mean."

"Well, that's the deal. You either work or you pay, so unless you're hiding a small fortune in that duffel bag of yours, I'm afraid so." Stanley could tell he was nervous about working. Starting your first job was hard enough without being surrounded by people decades older than you.

"It's no big deal. Just do what you're told," Stanley told him. "Sometime this weekend we'll go down to the restaurant so you can see where you'll be working. That way you can meet Amato . . . He takes some getting used to."

Cooper sat up. "What do you mean?"

"He's . . . Well, he's loud. You'll see. Don't worry about it, though" Stanley said. "Besides, you're a volunteer not an employee. It's not the same thing. I'm pretty sure there's a rule against throwing things at volunteers."

Noticing the alarmed look on Cooper's face, he tried to downplay the very real possibility that Amato would throw something at him. "If he throws anything, it'll probably just be a spoon or something. No big deal. . . . I'm kidding . . . mostly. It has to be better than school, right?"

Cooper nodded. "I guess so."

School was mostly why Cooper was spending the summer with him. According to his mom, Cooper didn't have many friends, and no close ones, and his grades had been steadily going downhill since he'd entered his freshman year of high school. Cooper could do the work, his teachers told her, but he missed so many classes that it was impossible for him to keep up. What he did when he wasn't in class, she didn't know, but she was afraid he was going to start hanging out with the kind of kids who never went to class and smoked cigarettes or worse. There was also the very real possibility that he wouldn't graduate on time if he didn't start turning things around.

"Look on the bright side," Stanley said. "You get to spend the whole summer soaking up the wisdom of your elders."

Cooper didn't say anything.

"Okay," Stanley said. "How about this: You get to spend the whole summer away from the kids at your high school."

Cooper seemed to mull it over. "Okay," he said.

"That's better," Stanley said, and then thought of something suddenly. Pointing at Cooper's phone, he said, "Does that thing have an alarm on it?"

Chapter Three

"That kid's got some scowl on him," Ned said.

Cooper was out in the parking lot performing various tricks on his skateboard. He didn't look like he was having much fun.

"I'm thinking we should take him to the track with us tomorrow," Stanley said.

The Last Stop as a community had been going to opening day at Arapaho Park since the early nineties. Once a year they all piled into four transport buses and made the two hour commute to witness the most exciting two minutes in sports. It was something Stanley and Ned looked forward to all year. Stanley doubted that Cooper had ever seen a horse race, even though California had two of the premier tracks in the country.

"Jesus, I almost forgot," Ned said. "Don't let me forget to wear my lucky hat."

"Maybe if you leave your hat home this year, you'll come back with some money."

Even though Cooper didn't seem to be enjoying himself, Stanley was glad he was off his phone and outside. They'd spent the previous day and most of the evening sitting in silence. Stanley didn't generally watch much television, but it was something they could do together without Stanley feeling like he needed to fill the air with a bunch of annoying questions. The only break had come when Stanley caught Ned peeking in the front-room window. Surprisingly, this wasn't the first time it had happened. Ned liked to entertain himself in creative ways, one of which was trying to give Stanley a heart attack by banging on the window when Stanley was watching television. Now, it appeared he was going to up his game now that Cooper was here. It backfired, though, when Cooper caught Ned's reflection in the television screen and wheeled around. Ned acted like he was inspecting the window frame and then scampered off.

A few minutes later, the doorbell rang, and Stanley found Ned on the other side of the door.

Speaking too loudly, Ned said, "Sorry, Stanley, but it appears your window needs replacing."

"Is that so," Stanley said. "Inspect a lot of windows these days?"

Ned didn't answer and brushed by him and approached Cooper.

"So, who's the little fellow?"

Stanley cringed.

"You shouldn't spy on people," Cooper said.

"What?" Ned said, turning to Stanley. "What is he talking about?"

"You heard him," Stanley said.

"All right, all right, so I was having a little fun. Sue me." Ned nodded at Cooper. "Is that your skateboard?"

"No, it's mine," Stanley said

"Hysterical," Ned said. "I used to ride a skateboard way back. Was pretty good, too. Maybe we can go boarding together sometime. Of course, I'd have to get a skateboard somewhere."

The grimace on Cooper's face seemed genuine.

"Right," Stanley said. "And then we can rush you off to the emergency room."

Ned mulled it over for a minute. "Yeah, you're probably right."

"You can have mine if you want it," Cooper said. "It's a piece of junk."

This surprised Stanley. When Cooper had been approached by Marcus in the lobby, he'd seemed pretty attached to it. Ned picked up the skateboard and held it at arm's length.

"Oh, it's not so bad," he said. "The scull is pretty neat."

"Nobody rides fat boards anymore," Cooper said, standing up. "You see these rail things and the skid plate? Nobody has these anymore. Nobody has had these for like a million years. The wheels are too wide, the bearings are slow, the trucks are too loose and you can't even tighten them. I don't know how I'm ever supposed to get good on this thing."

Stanley didn't know what to say. It was the most words Cooper had strung together since he'd arrived.

"Well, Christmas will be coming around before you know it—" Stanley tried to stop Ned from continuing this line of advice, but he wasn't fast enough. "Why don't you ask Santa Claus for a new one?"

All the life seemed to be sucked out of Cooper and he flopped back down on the couch. Stanley shook his head and rubbed his temples.

"Don't you have somewhere to be?" Stanley asked him.

After Ned left, it had been pretty much nonstop reruns of Dragnet, which Stanley loved, but he doubted that Cooper did. Twice he asked him if he wanted to watch something else, and twice Cooper said that he didn't care, so they settled in. At six o'clock, Stanley heated up a batch of precooked hot dogs and chicken noodle soup and they ate in silence. At nine-thirty, Stanley got Cooper a blanket and pillow out of the closet and turned in.

In the morning, Holy Moses once again lightened the mood. Ms. Crocker from across the hall had a habit of going out early in the morning and feeding the squirrels and the birds and whatever other wildlife happened to show up. She was out there again, and Cooper was watching her. Or, more accurately, he was watching Holy Moses trying to sneak up on one of the squirrels she was feeding. He wasn't doing a very good job of being sneaky. When he got within ten feet, the squirrel bolted for the trees, chattering angrily as he went. Holy barked and bounded after him, startling Ms. Crocker, who inadvertently threw all the remaining nuts up in the air. "Oh, Holy!" she yelled, as he ran by her. "You big lug!"

Cooper had smiled then, and even laughed a little, but it was short-lived. He spent the next hour playing a game on his phone, before finally asking if he could go outside and ride his skateboard.

So that's where they were now. Stanley had stopped by Ned's room so he'd have someone to talk to while Cooper was doing his thing. Stanley thought Cooper was pretty good, cheap skateboard or not. His favorite trick seemed to be approaching a curb and hopping his board, turning it ninety degrees in the air, then landing half on and half off the curb. It took him a few tries, but he eventually got it.

"Good job, kid!" Ned yelled and offered him a thumbs up.

Cooper ignored him.

"I hate to say it," Ned said, "but I sort of hope he falls."

"You're just upset because he caught you peeking in the window."

"Whatever," Ned said, putting his hands behind his head, leaning back and closing his eyes. "If he gets hit by a car or something, wake me up."

A minute later, Ned said, "How long do we have to be out here?"

"You don't have to be out here at all," Stanley said. "I

thought you were sleeping?"

"Who can sleep with all the racket? Let's go in and play darts or something. He'll be fine."

"And leave him out here by himself?"

"He's fifteen," Ned said, "not six. You afraid he's going to run away?"

"And ride his skateboard all the way back to California?"

"Then let's go do something else, he'll be—oh, here he comes. Act like you're sleeping."

Cooper skated up to them, kicked his board in the air, caught it and sat down next to them in the grass.

"You're pretty good at that," Stanley told him. "Thought you said you weren't any good."

"I didn't say that. I'd be better if I had my Naked."

"Excuse me?" Ned said, leaning forward. "I don't think you'd do any better if you were naked."

Stanley didn't have any idea what Cooper was talking about, either, but he was pretty sure Cooper wasn't talking about skateboarding naked.

"It's a kind of deck," Cooper told him.

Ned shook his head. "You lost me. You're going to skate naked on a deck?"

Cooper flopped down in the grass and flung his head around in mock exasperation, or maybe it was real.

"Okay," Cooper said, sitting up. "This," he said, holding up the skateboard, "is a deck."

"It's not a skateboard?" Ned asked.

Cooper sighed. "This," he said, knocking on the top of the board, "is a deck. When it doesn't have wheels and trucks on it, it's just a deck."

"Wait, wait, wait," Ned said. "What does skateboarding have to do with trucks?"

Stanley could tell that Ned was transitioning from genuinely confused to purposely aggravating Cooper.

"Never mind," Stanley said. "Go on."

"This is the problem with this skateboard," Cooper said. "When you buy it, it's all together. You pull it out of the box and it's good to go."

"That's not a good thing?" Stanley asked.

"No. First you pick out the deck you want. Then you decide on the trucks—these things," Cooper said, pointing to the things the wheels were attached to. "Okay? Then you pick out your risers, and then your wheels, and then your bearings and your grip tape. Then you put it all together."

"Seems like a hassle," Ned said. "Especially when you can get one straight out of the box."

"He wants it custom," Stanley said. "How much does all this cost?"

"For what I want? About a hundred."

"Whew!" Ned said. "Back when I was boarding—"

"Nobody calls it that anymore," Cooper reminded him.

"Mine cost five bucks," Ned said.

"That was a hundred years ago," Stanley said.

"I don't know, kid," Ned said. "Seems pretty expensive, especially if you're going to ride it naked. Though, come to think of it, we were darn near naked when we were boarding—"

"Nobody calls it that anymore!" Cooper and Stanley said in unison.

"But we didn't do tricks," Ned continued, ignoring them. "We mostly went down hills like we were surfing. Ever try that?"

"No," Cooper said. "But even if I wanted to, I couldn't. Watch . . ."

Cooper set the skateboard down and propelled it down the sidewalk. They watched as the board veered hard left, jumped the curb and started down the hill towards the main entrance. They all noticed, more or less simultaneously, that Eva Parks was roaring up the drive in the Corvette she'd won up at the casinos a few years ago. She was too scared to drive it on regular streets, but she liked to periodically do laps around the property. It was obvious she didn't see the skateboard. Stanley and Ned saw the futility in trying to stop the inevitable, but Cooper had the invincibility of youth on his side, and dashed after it, waving his hands in the air. Cooper might have managed to reach the skateboard before it passed underneath the driver's side front tire, but he tripped before he could get there, hitting the ground hard and sliding along the rough surface. Stanley and Ned both winced.

"That had to hurt," Ned said.

"Come on, let's go see if he's all right."

Eva screeched to a halt, and seeing Cooper laid out in the street, assumed, logically enough, that she had just run him down. When she got out of the car, she had both hands covering her mouth and she was making a strange mewing noise. When she took her hands away from her mouth, it turned out that she was saying, "Oh, my," over and over again. It wasn't until Cooper hopped up and picked up his broken skateboard, that they were able to convince her that she hadn't committed vehicular homicide. Cooper's pant-leg was torn and there was a fair amount of blood, but he was obviously going to be fine.

"Tough break," Ned said.

Cooper seemed more concerned about his skateboard than he was about his leg.

"Well," Stanley said. "Let's go get that cleaned up."

Cooper said it was fine.

Ned put his arm around Cooper's shoulder and said, "It might be fine now, but if it gets infected they'll have to cut your leg off."

CHAPTER FOUR

To Marie Chord, there were few things scarier than a blank piece of paper. The fact that she'd chosen a typewriter as her instrument of choice when she'd decided to become a writer wasn't helping things. There was something about the physical paper sticking out of the typewriter that made her feel like a real writer, but it was also a lot more intimidating, probably because it felt so permanent. She knew how to use the computers in the library, but writing on a screen felt strange to her, less real. She was also paranoid that she'd hit a wrong button and all her work would be wiped out and she'd have to start over again.

She had purposely put her writing desk on the wall opposite the television set. That way she wouldn't be tempted to turn on the afternoon Soaps while she was working. This was proving to be a non-issue because she'd spent less than fifteen minutes at her writing desk in the last week. She'd spent a lot of time looking at it, though. In her defense, she hadn't turned on Days of Our Lives, either. She viewed this as a suitable punishment for not having the willpower to sit at her desk and work.

She'd read that putting your writing desk by a window was a bad idea, too, because you'd likely get lost gazing at a tree or something. It turned out that she didn't have to be sitting at a desk to get lost looking out the window. This morning, Stanley, her neighbor from down the hall, was outside with another man she sometimes saw around but had never talked to. They were sitting on one of the benches watching a young man, a teenager, probably, riding his skateboard. Younger people often visited, but they didn't usually stay long enough to bring along recreational things.

She'd noticed them out there right after her morning coffee, which was the worst possible timing because that's when she was supposed to be sitting down at her desk to write. She'd read that starting a story was the hardest part. As far as she was concerned, that was bunk. She had all sorts of beginnings. It was everything that came after the beginning that had her stumped. The twenty-or-so books on writing she'd read over the last six months talked endlessly about hooking the reader in the beginning and satisfying the reader with an inevitable, clever ending, but they said very little about the stuff in the middle. She was great at coming up with fun, provocative first sentences. Talking trees had shown up three times, and a three-legged dog had shown up twice, but all he did was hobble around, trying to figure out how to lift his other leg to go to the bathroom. She'd even managed to kill someone in a first sentence: "The kill-shot came just as Trenton was zipping up his fly." That was one of her favorites because it was edgy and gave her an opportunity to use "kill-shot," which she had come across in a book about writing crime fiction, but, so far, nothing had come of that one, either.

She read all the books on writing she could get her hands on: Mystery Writing, Travel Writing, Writing in Your Spare Time, Writing Simply, Writing Your Dreams, Horror Writing Secrets, Your New Six-Figure Writing Income! Her favorite was, "Write Now!" which she had been quietly ignoring since she'd first read it. Somehow, disregarding the shouting book title made her feel strong. Sometimes when she was alone and came across the title on her bookshelf, she'd say, "Don't tell me what to do," and then have a celebratory cocktail.

She'd been collecting other books, too. Books with titles like: "Change Your Life with Twelve Easy Steps!" and "Get Up!" That one she purposely placed on her nightstand so she could disregard that one, too. A common theme in these books was the need to take action. You could do all the planning in the world, they said, but if you never took action, you'd never get anywhere. She particularly liked a quote from Emerson that often appeared in these books: "Do the thing and you'll have the power," Emerson advised, but she changed it to, "Do the freaking thing and you'll have the freaking power!" She liked her version better because it had a condescending, hateful quality that Emerson never intended.

"All right, Marie," she told herself just this morning. "If you want to write, sit down and write. Don't make a big production of it." This was a common pep talk she gave herself most mornings. But like those other times, as she approached her desk, she suddenly veered off course and found herself in the kitchen cleaning out the freezer. In the ten or twelve seconds it had taken her to get there, she'd come up with a three-part story about why the freezer needed to be cleaned and organized immediately. Maybe she was avoiding her desk because her last writing effort had produced this gem: "The wind rushed through the open window hotly," which was so bad it made her want to cry.

Her friends weren't much help, either. She'd made the mistake of telling them how she was going to spend her golden years penning bestsellers in multiple genres, so now every time they saw her, one of them would ask her how the book was coming. "Oh, it's coming," she'd say, which she figured wasn't exactly untrue. It was coming, she was sure of it. It just hadn't made it to paper yet. Last week, one of these conversations took a more serious turn when Florence casually mentioned how she'd write a book, too, if she ever found the time, as if time was the only factor, and Marie excused herself and left before she said or did something she couldn't take back.

By the time she was done cleaning out and organizing the freezer, she was so disgusted with herself that she said, "Oh, for god's sake, Marie!" out loud and marched to her writing desk and sat down before she could talk herself out of it. She replaced the blank piece of paper in the typewriter with a fresh one, centered it, took a deep breath, and then wrote, "The hot wind rushed in through the door left ajar by her cat, Frances."

She leaned back and sighed, only half disgusted with what she'd written. It wasn't much better than her previous efforts, but at least there was something other than hot wind. The three-legged dog hadn't shown up, either, which she thought was promising. But most importantly, there was a cat named Frances. She was going to write more, but the sound of screeching breaks broke her concentration. She didn't hear a crash or anything, so she returned to her work and reread the sentence again. It had potential, she decided, so rather than ruin it with any additional words, Marie decided to knock off for the day, thereby ending her first truly successful writing day. Tomorrow she'd set about finding out who Francis was and where he was going.

She returned to the window to see what Stanley and the other two were up to, but they were gone. She was just turning around when she heard a soft knock on her door. It wasn't the staff. They wouldn't be nearly so quiet about it. When she cautiously opened the door, she surprisingly found Stanley, his friend, and the boy standing in front of her. She was going to comment about how she'd been watching them, but the boy looked moody, so she said, "Yes?" instead.

"Sorry to bother you, Marie," Stanley said. "Do you

have a First Aid kit?"

Marie had been running possible scenarios through her head about why these three would suddenly be outside her door, but the need of a First Aid kit wasn't one of them.

"He fell down chasing his skateboard and almost got run over by Eva in her Corvette," Stanley said, pointing at the kid.

"So, that's what I heard!" Marie said. "Well, that is something!"

"I don't have any bandages or anything and there's no one at the nurses' station," Stanley said.

"I suppose I probably have something," Marie said, quickly adding, "You all stay here. I'll be back in a minute."

She felt bad about not welcoming them in, but the piece of paper with her only promising line on it was still sticking out of the typewriter, and she didn't want them accidentally reading it. You couldn't read something like that without then asking a bunch of awkward questions.

She started for the bathroom. She paused and looked back, making sure they hadn't disregarded her request before turning down the hall and disappearing into the bathroom. She had some stuff for cuts, but she knew from personal experience that this particular brand stung like the dickens. It was better than nothing. She'd just have to make sure she warned him. The only bandages she had were the small round ones.

"You okay in there?" She presumed that the voice belonged to Stanley's friend.

Marie closed the medicine cabinet and hurried back to the front room. To her surprise, she found Stanley and the kid sitting on her sofa, and, to her horror, she found the other one sitting at her writing desk.

"Show her your leg, Cooper," Stanley said. The kid, Cooper, reluctantly pulled his pant leg up and exposed a three inch square patch of road rash. He was trying to convince Stanley that he wasn't hurt, but he wasn't doing a very good job of it.

"You'll be saying that right up until the time they cut your leg off," Stanley's friend said, which she found alarming, but no one else seemed to.

"Would you stop saying that, Ned?" Stanley said, but Ned's attention had turned to Marie's typewriter. Before she could stop him, he had pulled the paper out and was trying to find the right distance and angle to be able to read what she'd typed.

"I really wish you wouldn't read that," Marie said, almost pleading, but Ned managed to contort himself into a position to make out the type and read, out loud, "The hot wind rushed in through the door left ajar by her cat, Francis . . ."

Marie sat down, defeated, in the sitting chair next to the couch. "I really wish you wouldn't have read that," she said.

"Really, Ned?" Stanley said.

Ned ignored them. "It's good stuff," he said. "But where did he go?"

"Who?"

"The cat."

"I have no idea," Marie said. "It's just something silly I wrote."

"I wish I could write," Ned said. "Must be something to be able to pull stuff out of thin air."

Marie laughed self-consciously.

"I'm serious," Ned said. "Think about it. Before you came along, Francis the cat didn't even exist."

Marie couldn't bring herself to look at him, but she smiled down at her hands.

"I don't mean to interrupt," Stanley said. "But I don't want him to bleed—"

"Oh!" Marie said. "I totally forgot!"

Instead of handing them the medication, Marie scooted towards Cooper, opened the bottle and began jabbing at Cooper's wound with the little applicator.

"Jesus!" Cooper said, startling all three of them by how loud he said it.

"Thought you said you weren't hurt," Ned said.

"Oh, boy," Marie said. "I should have warned you. It does sting, doesn't it?" Marie quickly stuck one of the bandages on his knee, wincing a little when she realized that it only covered about half of it and that all the sticky parts were directly on the wound. It was going to be a howler when he tried to take it off.

The three of them stood up. She didn't make eye contact with Cooper.

"Sorry to bother you, Marie," Stanley said. "We'll get going now."

"Hey!" Ned said suddenly. "Maybe he's running away from home."

"What?" Stanley said.

"The cat. Maybe he's running away from something."

Marie smiled. "Maybe."

"Say thank you, Cooper," Stanley said.

"Thank you," Cooper said, but it didn't sound like he meant it. She couldn't say she blamed him.

"You're very welcome," Marie said, but she was still looking at Ned.

CHAPTER FIVE

"Kid's having a rough first few days," Ned said. "You think this was a good idea bringing him here to meet Amato? He's already nervous. Once he meets who he's working for, he might run screaming from the building."

"I think it would be worse not knowing what you're walking into," Stanley said. "Besides, he's volunteering, he's not working. Amato should go easy on him . . ." This sounded logical, but Stanley wasn't sure he believed it. Going easy didn't seem to be in Amato's nature.

Cooper wasn't around to hear any of this. The three of them had come for lunch so Cooper could get a feel for where he'd be spending most of his time and who'd he'd be working for, but Cooper had made a beeline for the bathroom as soon as they'd arrived.

Ned swiveled his body around so he could see the bathrooms.

"You know what he's doing in there, don't you?" Ned said. "Smoking grass."

"Oh, please."

"Think about it. What else would he be doing that would take this long? He's probably in there with the door locked and the window cracked, toking away."

As if on cue, the bathroom door suddenly swung open and Cooper started his slow, moody shuffle back to the table.

"Good lord," Ned said. "At this rate we'll have finished eating and paid the check before he gets here."

Cooper's lack of urgency under all circumstances was a sticking point with Stanley, too, but he found himself saying to Ned, "He's fifteen. Cut him some slack."

A minute later, Cooper slid into the booth next to Ned. Their food had arrived and Cooper started in on his hamburger as only a fifteen year old boy can: With both hands and with little pause for chewing. Ned turned towards him and leaned in, sniffing the air around him.

"What?" Cooper said.

"Looks like you got the munchies," Ned said. "Everything go all right in there?" Ned now focused on Cooper's eyes to see if he was squinting. "Thought maybe you were trying to jimmy open the window or something—"

Cooper started to reply, but he was interrupted by the kitchen door suddenly banging open and one of the busboys storming out, untying his apron as he went. When he passed them, he swung his apron over his head like a cowboy with a rope and let it fly back towards the kitchen.

From the kitchen they heard the unmistakable voice of Chef Amato yelling after him, "You quit! You quit! No, no! You fired! That's what you are!"

Cooper sat blinking at the kitchen. When Amato came roaring out of the kitchen, Cooper visibly recoiled. Amato saw the three of them sitting there and came over and placed both of his large hands on the table and looked back and forth between Stanley and Ned, not bothering to look at Cooper.

"This is what I say to him: when there are no tables to clean, you do dishes. If there are no dishes, you mop and wipe down the kitchen. If this is done, you find me and I tell you what to do next. Understand? Of course. A baby can understand this. But are there dishes to do? Yes. Does he do them? No. Did he mop? No. Did he wipe down the kitchen? No. Does he come see me? No. What does he do? He holds up the wall with his stupid body like he is waiting for a bus. All day I find him leaning. So I say to him, 'Work! Work!' Does he listen? No. He says I am a slave-driver and a mean person, so I hit him with a bag of sugar . . . Is this so bad? Anyway, he is gone for good. Idiot."

When Amato was addressing you it was clear that your input wasn't needed, expected, or wanted, so none of them said anything, just nodded. After a moment of studying them, Amato changed gears. He said, "The chicken sandwich is good today, eh?"

Both Stanley and Ned had gotten the chicken sandwich, and it was indeed good and they told him so. Amato turned his attention to Cooper. "And what do we have here?" he asked. It was hard to say whether he was talking about Cooper or the hamburger.

"This is my grandson," Stanley said. "He's going to be helping you out for the summer."

"Me? Here?" Amato waggled his index finger and shook his head. "Of course he's not working here. What can he do? He's so small I barely saw him there. What can a small boy like him do for me?"

"They were supposed to tell you all this," Stanley said. "He's volunteering his time . . . You're supposed to know all this."

"I know nothing. Anyway, it's no good."

"Your busboy just quit," Ned reminded him.

"Not quit. Fired!"

"Yes, well. You need the help."

"Nathan will clean the tables."

Nathan was five or six years older than Cooper and had been working there close to four years. Even though his title was Assistant Chef, up until recently he'd only been trusted to cook the hash browns and toast the bread. He spent the rest of his time doing whatever Amato ordered him to do. Mostly he fetched various ingredients and cooking utensils, not unlike a nurse assisting a surgeon.

"Nathan has better things to do than cleaning tables," Stanley said. "Cooper can handle it."

"No good."

Stanley then suggested that Cooper help him prepare the food, but this was met with such loud, angry laughter and finger waggling that they quickly worked their way down the restaurant employee food chain.

"Let him wash the dishes," Ned said.

Amato snorted. "And have him breaking my glasses? No."

Cooper shifted nervously in his seat.

"He can mop the floors," Ned suggested. "You can mop the floors, can't you, kid?"

Cooper turned to Stanley for help, but Stanley was waiting for an answer, too. "I guess so," Cooper said.

"See there," Amato said. "He guesses. I don't like guesses. People who guess at things can't be trusted to change the mop water when it gets dirty."

"Oh, for god's sake, Amato," Stanley said. He knew how difficult Amato could be, but this was getting ridiculous. "If you don't trust him, have him seat the customers."

"And what will they think when they are greeted by a slovenly riff raff?"

Cooper shifted in his seat again.

"Look at him," Amato continued. "With his hair in his eyeballs he'll be running into things . . . Let me think! There must be something for the little riff raff to do . . . I have it! He will sweep. I will give him a broom and he will sweep. But he must promise not to trip my customers. Can he comprehend this?"

Stanley turned to Cooper, whose face was bright red either from embarrassment or anger.

"Well, Cooper," Stanley said. "Can you comprehend this?"

"I guess," Cooper said.

Chapter Six

"Today is the day, Stanley!" Ned said. "I can feel it!" Ned said this every time they went to the track. All during the two hour trip, Ned told Stanley and Cooper about how they were going to have to rent another vehicle to transport all the money he was going to win.

This was all part of the fun. The bus was full and even Randy, the driver, seemed excited about the upcoming day, even though he was disappointed that he wasn't allowed to take part in the two dollar beers at the track. For most of the other residents, opening day was an event, not unlike a parade or a concert. The thought of actually making money didn't occur to most of them. Ned, on the other hand, and to a much lesser extent, Stanley, were hyper aware of all the money floating around in the various pools, and if they said they weren't interested in getting a piece of it, they were lying. It didn't happen often, but there had been a handful of years when one or both of them had come back with more money than they had gone with. If there was any profit, they usually ended up spending it on hot dogs and beer.

Unlike Stanley, Ned only had two kinds of plays: either

there was a horse with a name too juicy to ignore, like *Massive Riches* or *Sky's the Limit*, or he bet the favorite to Show. Betting the favorite to come in either first, second or third, was, bar none, the dumbest wager you could make at the track, and one that Ned placed over and over again, despite Stanley's constant scolding. And when Ned would strut off to the ticket window to collect $2.20 on his $2.00 wager, Stanley just shook his head. There was no getting through to him. The fact was that Ned was more interested in cashing tickets than he was in making actual money. This is what made Ned's constant chatter about having to have armed guards escort him to the bus so he wouldn't be mugged of all his winnings, all the more ridiculous.

By the time they pulled up to the track entrance and piled out, Stanley was trying not to hit Ned with his rolled up notebook.

Even though Cooper hadn't said much on the drive down, he seemed content with spending the day at the track. The first thing Stanley was going to do was buy Cooper one of the famous track hot dogs and a large nacho with extra jalapenos. It just wasn't the same if you didn't leave a little bit sick to your stomach, either from too many beers and too much sun, or too much track food and not enough water. Of course, if you lost a bunch of money, you'd feel pretty sick, too, but Cooper wasn't going to have that problem. He was too young to gamble, even if he had his own money, but Stanley planned on placing some bets for him if he showed any interest.

"Luck is in the air!" Ned said, dramatically inhaling through his nose. "Do you feel it, Coop?"

"Don't call him that," Stanley said.

"I don't feel anything," Cooper said.

"Don't worry about it," Stanley told him. "I don't feel anything, either."

After getting in and buying the racing program, they

found a little picnic table twenty-or-so feet from the rail to sit and eat and wait for the races to begin. Stanley was a little disappointed that Cooper didn't want to try one of the hot dogs, opting for a king-sized bag of peanut M&M's instead. Ned thought he was crazy for this and said so, ordering an extra hot dog just in case Cooper changed his mind. Even though Cooper wasn't partaking in all the track had to offer, Stanley could tell he was interested. When the horses and jockeys came out on the track for the first race, he was transfixed.

Stanley and Ned settled down and began scanning the past performances for the day's races. Ned noticed The Hustler Hathaway seated at one of the picnic tables by herself, making notes in a little notebook. Stanley had watched her on the bus. She had printed out the past performances on one of the computers in the library and had spent the trip down studying them intently. Every so often she'd smile and highlight something. Stanley would have given his left arm to see her methods. It was common knowledge that making money on horse racing was next to impossible, but apparently no one had given Ms. Hathaway the memo. The truth was that if you were a good enough handicapper and could spot situations and angles that the betting public missed, you could make a lot of money. Not surprisingly, Ms. Hathaway had a knack for this. All of this irritated Ned, who had once accused her of using voodoo rituals and various incantations before coming to the track. Of course, this didn't stop him from trying to look over her shoulder when she was making notes in her program every chance he got.

"Not today, Hathaway!" Ned yelled over his shoulder. "Today is my day!"

Stanley, who was facing Ms. Hathaway, saw her roll her eyes and wave him off with a fluttering of her fingers.

"What did she do?" Ned asked.

"Oh, I think you rattled her."

"You bet I did!" Ned said, returning to his program. After a moment, Ned suddenly stood up and thrust his program in Stanley's face. "Look at that!"

"Look at what?" Stanley said. "I can't see anything with you waving it all over the place."

Ned suddenly realized that he was making a scene, and quickly sat back down and slid his chair in and leaned over the table.

"Now, don't say anything," Ned whispered, "but look at the eighth race."

Stanley did. Nothing jumped out at him.

"Look at the number four horse," Ned said. Stanley did as he was told, but found nothing remarkable. The horse had been running at this class level. His speed figures were in line with the other runners. His form seemed okay, but nothing to get excited about.

"Really!" Ned said. "Look at his name!"

"*Bet the Farm*," Stanley read.

"Exactly. That is what I'm going to do. What do you think, Cooper?"

Cooper had been watching the exchange with a comical mixture of bewilderment and amusement. "You don't have a farm," he said, and Stanley laughed out loud.

Ned waved him off. "This is what we do," he said. "We pool our money together. We go all-in on *Bet the Farm* to Show. We'll be millionaires!"

Stanley shook his head.

"A name like that and you don't want in!" Ned said, clearly flabbergasted.

"He's three to one, Ned," Stanley said. "He'll probably go lower than that by post-time, but you go right ahead."

"That's why we need to pool our money together. It's a sure thing!"

Cooper had gotten up and wandered over to the rail. The horses and jockeys were making the slow walk to the starting gate. Ned decided to use this time to educate him on the art of evaluating a horse's current conditioning. "Now," Ned said, "when they're walking by, pay real close attention. They might look good on paper, but if they don't look right before the race . . . No good. It's all in the eyes. If their eyes are clear and their ears are pricked up, that's a good sign. If their coats are sweaty and their eyes are darting all over the place and they look rank, that's no good. High strung horses can't be trusted to run. Now, if one of them makes eye contact with you—"

Before Ned could finish the thought, the five horse, *Ain't He Something*, suddenly stopped, swung his head toward Cooper, then slowly walked over to him. It was obvious after a moment that what the horse was interested in wasn't so much Cooper as it was the package of M&M's he was eating, but Ned could hardly contain himself.

"What are you waiting for?" Ned said. "Give him your M&M's!"

Cooper spilled a few into his hand and offered them to *Ain't He Something*, who took them and happily munched them down before his jockey directed him back towards the others making their way to the starting gate. *Ain't He Something* complied, but not without a couple of reluctant glances over his shoulder at Cooper.

Ned was speechless, but so excited that he was nearly jumping up and down. "Cooper! Stanley! Coop—Did you see that? Did—Now we run!"

"Run?" Cooper said.

Ned grabbed him by the shirt. "We've only got a few minutes until post-time!" Ned said. "What just happened was the Holy Grail! You bet on that horse, he'll win just for you." Ned snatched his racing program from the table and quickly thumbed through it until he came to *Ain't He Something*'s running lines.

"Fifteen to one!" Ned said. "Stanley! Give me all your money."

"Nope."

"Hurry! We don't have time!"

Stanley reluctantly gave him a ten dollar bill, but noticing the look of excitement in Cooper's eyes, added another twenty.

Stanley watched as Ned and Cooper ran to the betting window. He couldn't help getting caught up in the excitement, even if Ned's reasoning was ridiculous. Ned was forever finding reasons to bet on horses. This one, he had to admit, was a better reason than most. It wasn't often that a racehorse came over to the rail for a visit, no matter what the reason. And if the horse happened to win, it would be quite a story.

Stanley took the few minutes before the race began to look at the fifth race and found a horse named *Fools Gold* who was coming off a long layoff but who was trained by the tracks top trainer and was switching to a better jockey. He was also posting blazing workout times. He was ten to one on the morning-line; a ridiculously good price for a horse with so many things going for him.

Ned and Cooper returned to the table just as the horses were being loaded into the starting gate. "Who you got there?" Ned asked, looking at the name of the horse Stanley had circled in his program. Ned nudged Cooper in the side. "Who bets on a horse with a name like *Fools Gold*?"

Stanley ignored him and looked at the tote board. "*Ain't He Something*'s twenty to one," he said.

"Didn't I tell you today was the day?" Ned said. "Twenty to one and we've got sixty-three dollars on him to win!" Ned said. Stanley was surprised. Ned almost never bet a horse strictly to win.

Ned and Cooper went to the rail so they could yell their horse home, and Stanley joined them.

A moment after they reached the rail, the horses burst from the starting gate and the track announcer informed them that *Ain't He Something* had jumped out to an early three length lead going into the first turn. It was hard to see because the horses were on the far side of the track, but by the time they rounded the second turn and were starting down the stretch, they didn't need the track announcer anymore. They could clearly see that *Ain't He Something* had extended his lead to over ten lengths.

Ned yelled and began jumping up and down, waving his lucky hat over his head. Stanley couldn't help banging his rolled up racing program against his leg, the way he always did when his horse was on the verge of winning. Cooper got caught up in the excitement, too, waving his bag of M&M's over his head and yelling, "He's going to win! He's going—" But as the horses approached, *Ain't He Something* abruptly started angling out towards them. When he cleared the lane of horses behind him, *Ain't He Something* slowed to a trot, despite his jockey leaning virtually sideways in the saddle, desperately trying to urge him back into the race. *Ain't He Something* stopped in front of Cooper and gently snatched his bag of M&M's. Then he turned and continued the race at a leisurely, happy gallop.

After announcing the winner and runner-ups, the track announcer offered a play-by-play of *Ain't He Something* as he loped along to the finish. When he crossed the finish line, the crowd roared with laughter. *Ain't He Something*'s jockey decided to make the most of it and waved his hat over his head and bowed. In all his years of coming to the races, Stanley had never seen anything like it. Ned was beside himself, turning first to Cooper and then to Stanley and then back again. He stopped just short of throwing his lucky hat on the ground and stomping on it. Cooper thought the whole thing was funny.

"You and those silly M&M's just cost us like a million dollars!" Ned said. It would have been nowhere near a million dollars, but it would have been a nice chunk of change. The story, on the other hand, was priceless. Ned would eventually get over it. Stanley tried to lessen the blow by giving him the rest of his hot dog, but this, too, backfired when Ned squirted mustard all over the front of his shirt.

"Look on the bright side," Stanley said. "You still have *Bet the Farm* in the eighth."

"No I don't," Ned said, "I bet everything I had on . . . Him!" Ned pointed to the large screen showing a replay of the race. Ned didn't say anything, but when *Ain't He Something* took the M&M's from Cooper's hand, he had to laugh. "Yeah, he's something, all right," Ned said.

Behind them, The Hustler Hathaway quietly picked up her ticket and took it to the cashier.

CHAPTER SEVEN

"Well, Mr. Cooper?" Amato said. "Do I get you a broom, or do you go away?"

Cooper wanted more than anything to go away, but he knew he couldn't. Amato nodded and led him through the kitchen to a little closet next to the sinks and pointed to the broom.

"This is my favorite broom," Amato said, "so treat it well. You see how clean the bristles? This is how you return it. The pan, I don't care. It's yellow and ugly already, but the broom! Be careful!"

Cooper took the broom, but not seeing anything in the immediate area that needed sweeping, planted the bristles into the floor and leaned his weight on it, waiting for further instructions.

"For god's sake!" Amato shouted. "Does it look like a cane? Are you a cripple?"

Cooper immediately realized his error and flipped the broom over and began straightening out the bristles.

"Is this what you do?" Amato continued. "Someone gives you instructions and you insult them?"

Cooper began sweeping around Amato's feet.

"Out there!" Amato said, grasping Cooper by both shoulders and pointing him towards the door. "You go away from me now. I have dishes to prepare. Broom, broom! Just like a motor car, only different."

Cooper did as he was told, starting just outside the kitchen doors and working his way around the perimeter, making sure to get underneath all the tables. It was just after six in the morning and residents hadn't started arriving yet. He had made it halfway around the perimeter before he had enough dust to warrant using the dustpan. He felt silly. The place was already spotless: the chairs, the tables, the floors; even the walls and light fixtures looked brand new. If it wasn't for the occasional curses emanating from the kitchen, he'd almost describe the place as peaceful. A few times he stopped sweeping to look out one of the many windows, but then the banging in the kitchen would stop and Amato would yell, "Broom! Broom! young Cooper. Like a motor car, only less expensive!"

While Cooper wasn't happy about working in the restaurant, he had to admit that the smells that soon came wafting out of the kitchen were extraordinary. His mother was a master of macaroni and cheese and hot dogs, which made up the majority of his diet when he was home. That and cereal. Because of this, he'd never really craved food. Eating was just something that had to be done, like sleeping or going to the bathroom. But now, he found himself sweeping closer and closer to the kitchen, even though there was virtually nothing to sweep.

Cooper had never thought of old people as being hostile, but when they started filing in, he got an uneasy feeling. Everyone was curious who he was, that was obvious. A few of them stopped abruptly and did an about-face to get a better look at him, and when they did, they squinted in what Cooper perceived as a not-so-friendly manner. Others chuckled and shook their heads, which Cooper found even more disconcerting. Cooper felt so out of place that he kept his head down and continued his never ending rounds. The only time he looked up was to watch the waitresses bringing out the food. All he'd had to eat was a banana.

Mid morning, Amato came out to greet the patrons, walking up to each table and placing a hand on the shoulder of one of the diners and asking them, "Good, no?" and Cooper made sure to look busy.

The sweeping became so monotonous that when someone dropped a napkin or a crust of toast, Cooper became excited and rushed to pick it up. He turned it into a sort of game. It was during one of these attempted cleanups that he found himself nose to nose with Holy Moses. Up until then, he'd only seen Holy from a far. Now, up close and personal, Cooper realized that Holy was actually quite a bit bigger than he was if he stood up on his hind legs.

Now that he was within touching distance, Cooper had the overwhelming urge to smoosh Holy's cheeks together.

From somewhere behind him, a male voice said, "Only one person alive allowed to do that to Holy and that's—" Cooper never had a chance to find out who the man was talking about because before he knew what was happening, he was on his back and Holy had one enormous paw in the middle of his chest, pinning him to the floor. Cooper was too shocked to do anything but lay there. Again, Cooper heard the voice. This time, it said, "He'll let you up in a minute. It's that piece of cheese he wants. Just stay still until he's finished. He's not interested in hurting you. It would take too much energy."

He was right. Once Holy had finished the cheese, he sniffed Cooper's face then abruptly turned and walked away. A quiet laughter started at the tables nearest him and traveled throughout the restaurant. When Cooper sat up and looked back towards the kitchen, Amato was standing just outside the door. He had one hand on his hip, but he was smiling and waggling his index finger.

"He'll forgive you eventually." The voice, it turned out, belonged to a man sitting alone in the booth behind him. "You've got a check next to your name, though, so you've got a long road ahead of you."

"I don't think Amato will ever like me."

"I was talking about Holy Moses," the man said.

Cooper stood up slowly and retrieved his broom. He hadn't realized what a scene he'd caused until he pushed his hair out of his eyes and saw the thirty-or-so diners staring at him. The man in the booth said, "Once they realize you're not critically injured, they'll go back to their food. Can I give you a tip, son?"

Cooper nodded. He thought it best to keep his mouth shut.

"Lighten up a little bit. Until people get to know you, you're a curiosity, so smile and say hello. And when they don't answer, keep on smiling and saying hello. You'll wear them down eventually. But if you go around pushing your broom and avoiding eye contact, things are going to be rough."

The gentleman's suggestion to engage these people wasn't something Cooper was comfortable doing just yet. As he looked around, what he saw wasn't so much hostility as it was a sort of communal concern. He just wasn't so sure that the concern was for him.

After a moment, most of them returned to their meals. Holy Moses had wandered towards a booth in the corner where he was actively harassing the occupant for a bite of his toast.

Thankfully, the rest of the morning was uneventful. Anytime he saw a bit of food lying on the floor, he was sure to check Holy's whereabouts before picking it up. After the breakfast rush, he helped Nathan clear and wipe down the tables. Amato said he didn't want Cooper doing anything but sweeping, but as long as he was under Nathan's supervision, he didn't seem to mind. Nathan didn't say much, but after all the tables were cleared, he turned to him and said, "You better get back to sweeping." Then he smiled and added, "Broom, broom! Just like motor car, only doesn't need snow tires."

Cooper laughed. Nathan's imitation was spot-on.

At noon, Amato yelled for him. When Cooper got to the kitchen, he found Amato pointing to a plate with a club sandwich and fries on it.

"This is for you," Amato said. "You did okay so far. Holy didn't eat you, so you must not be too bad!" Amato handed him the plate. "Eat this," he said. "Then go outside and get some fresh air. Come back in one hour and sweep."

So that's what he did.

Chapter Eight

A few days later, Marie Chord found Cooper sitting in the grass leaning his back up against the east wall of the fitness center. She was on the path passing by when she noticed him. He looked troubled. She herself was troubled, which was why she had come out for a walk in the first place. She had thought that since she had written her first decent sentence that the rest would be smooth sailing. That was over a week ago, and she hadn't even managed to dip her toe in the water, let alone set sail. Every morning, she anticipated striding over to her writing desk with confidence, sitting down, and carrying on until lunch time, and every morning her old demons returned and held her back. She was so desperate that she tried to come up with ways of tricking herself into working. This morning, she made a deal with herself that if she wanted coffee, she'd have to drink it at her desk. She thought that if she just sat down, starting to work would be easy, but it turned out that if she sat down with a cup of coffee, all she did was drink the cup of coffee.

At eleven o'clock when she still hadn't written anything, she decided to go for a walk around the property. Most folks used the paths in the early mornings before the heat of the day kicked in, but she thought a little heat might do her good, so she put on her sun hat and sunglasses and headed out. She'd always liked walking. It was a good way to clear her head. It was also a good time to think. She brought a small notebook and a pen with her, just in case she was struck by the inspiration stick while she was out.

When Marie saw Cooper sitting there looking glum, she couldn't help but stop. "How's your knee?" she said, noticing that the bandage was gone.

Cooper looked at it. "Not too bad, I guess." These were the most words she had heard him string together, so she took it as an invitation to join him. She needed a break anyway. She'd been thinking hard about what Francis the cat was running from, but so far she hadn't come up with anything, and Cooper would serve as a welcome diversion.

"What are you up to today?" she asked.

"I've been helping out at the restaurant," Cooper said. "I'm on lunch break."

"Really? The restaurant, huh. Well, I can't imagine that's going very well," she said and wished she hadn't.

Cooper squinted up at her.

"Amato giving you a hard time?" she asked.

"I've been working there for three days and all he says is, 'Broom! Broom!'"

Marie laughed, then realized that Cooper didn't think it was nearly as funny. "Look," she said. "You don't have to be doing anything wrong to upset Amato. He was born upset. Have you met Nathan?"

"Sort of. He doesn't say much."

"Talk to Nathan. He'll teach you how to navigate him. Amato isn't really that mean, he's just loud. Watch him when he greets people, he's like a big teddy bear."

"He's been making me sandwiches."

"Well, there you go."

At that moment, they noticed Holy Moses across the

courtyard, smelling around a purple bush. He sneezed twice then laid down. When he noticed them watching him, his ears perked up and he sniffed the air, but he didn't get up.

"I don't think Holy Moses likes me much," Cooper said. "I was trying to pick up a piece of cheese the other morning and he pinned me to the floor."

Marie laughed. "Well, of course he did! You got between him and cheese. Let that be a lesson."

"I would have given it to him," Cooper said.

"Let me let you in on a little secret," Marie said. "Holy Moses runs this place. I know that must sound crazy, but Holy is like the cool kid at your school, the one everyone wants to be friends with. Most dogs pretty much love anything that doesn't hurt them, but with Holy, it's a little trickier. He has a way of sniffing out insincerity. He can spot a hollow note from down the hall and around the corner. He knows if you're a dog person, or if you're just trying to butter him up because you're afraid of him. He knows if you're genuine or not. It's uncanny. That's why people are drawn to him. You know why he loves Beverly so much? You've met Beverly, right, the receptionist?"

Cooper nodded.

"He loves her because she doesn't pretend to be anyone but herself. I have a theory. Let me know if I'm boring you. I think certain people carry around energy with them that Holy picks up on. Whether it's anger or bitterness or jealously, or just trying too hard to be liked or whatever it is, he senses it and I think it exhausts him. With Beverly or Harry, that's our maintenance man, he doesn't have to try to figure them out. They're right out in the open, the good the bad and the ugly. That's why I think he spends so much time with them."

"So you're saying I should try and get along with Holy Moses?" Cooper asked. "I should give him a dog bone or something?"

"No, Cooper," Marie said. "I'm saying you should be yourself, and getting along with Holy Moses will take care of itself."

Cooper noticed the notepad she was holding. "What's that?"

"Well," she said. "I'm writing a book . . . Sort of. I'm planning on writing a book. I want to write a book, let's put it that way."

"The cat, right?"

Marie laughed. "So you were paying attention, even when I was inflicting pain on you."

"What kind of book is it going to be?" Cooper asked.

"A novel."

"So, is it going to be true, or are you going to make it up?"

"It's going to be fiction, Cooper."

Cooper blinked.

"I'm going to make it up," she said. "What I have so far is a cat named Francis running away from home."

"Why would a cat run away from home?"

"Lord how I wish I knew that. I like the image, though. Every time I think about Francis, I picture him with a pack on his back and a little hobo hat and I crack myself up."

"Why would he be wearing a hat?"

"Because he's going to be a hobo," she said, shaking with inward laughter. "A hobo kitty."

Cooper looked confused and she laughed harder.

"Oh, Cooper, I wish you could see how funny that is. Maybe that's what I'll call the book, 'The Wild Adventures of a Hobo Kitty,'" she said. "Maybe the next book will be The Wild Adventures of a Three-legged dog."

Cooper smiled, but he didn't seem to get the absurdities of the titles. "I should probably get back," he said, but he didn't move.

Marie sensed his hesitation and thought she understood. "You're going to be all right, Cooper," Marie said.

Cooper pushed the hair out of his eyes and looked at her. "Yeah, I know," he said, "but he keeps yelling: Sweep!

Sweep! Broom! Broom!"

"And are you sweeping, or are you just sort of standing around?" Marie asked. "And be honest."

"I sweep for a while, but there's nothing to sweep so I get bored. What am I supposed to do, sweep imaginary things?"

"Yes, Cooper, that's what you're supposed to do. You smile, you nod, and you sweep imaginary things."

After Cooper said his goodbye and headed back across the courtyard, Marie opened her notebook and wrote: "Maybe Francis is running away from the three-legged dog???" and she smiled.

Chapter Nine

"Why are you back so early?" Stanley asked. Stanley was used to Cooper getting in around four o'clock and here it was barely noon.

Cooper didn't say anything. He brushed by Stanley and sat down on the couch.

"Did Amato give you the rest of the day off?"

"Something like that."

"What time do you go in tomorrow?"

"I don't."

"What do you mean you don't?"

"He told me to get out and not come back."

Stanley had been afraid something like this was going to happen, but it had been almost two weeks since Cooper had started. He thought he was out of the woods. Apparently not.

"So what happened?" Stanley asked. He was careful not to use an accusatory tone. He didn't want to automatically assume that Cooper had done something horrible. It was entirely possible that Amato was just drastically overreacting.

"He didn't like the way I did the dishes," Cooper said.

"I thought he wasn't going to let you wash the dishes."

"Well, now we know why."

Stanley wanted to get the whole story, so he told Cooper to stay put and headed down to the restaurant.

He found Amato in a surprisingly jovial mood. When Amato got upset about something, he tended to stay upset for long stretches, so he was surprised when Amato greeted him at the door and started explaining what happened before Stanley had a chance to ask.

"I gave him a good chance. I tell him to sweep. He does okay. Not great, but okay. Then he helps Nathan clear the tables. Again, he does okay. Not great, but nothing Nathan couldn't fix. I was starting to have high hopes. He is exceeding my low expectations of him, so I think to myself, 'What else can this helpless boy do?' I look and I see dishes piling up. It is not Nathan's fault. He is busy with other things. So I say, 'Young Cooper, stop your brooming! Do you think you can comprehend doing dishes?' He says he guesses. Everything with him is a guess. So I show him the sink and the dirty dishes and the racks and how to put them in the machine. Then I show him the big green button that means 'Go!' and the big red button that means 'Stop!' and I explain that he should never hit the red button unless the machine is going, 'Bang! Bang! Bang!' He nods so I show him the big sprayer and I ask him if he comprehends this and he says he guesses. Well, well, well! He guesses wrong! Dishes are too much for him. Instead of rinsing the dishes and getting all the chunky stuff off, he puts them straight into the machine! So what happens? This is what happens. The dishes come out the other side with dirty food burnt into them. Now I have meatloaf plates. I have cups with macaroni permanently stuck to them. I have forks that have turned red from dried ketchup! Who wants to eat off of a meatloaf plate and drink out of a macaroni cup? And now my machine goes, 'Bang! Bang! Bang!' even when there's nothing in it. Now poor Nathan will have to take it apart and fix it, all the while the dishes pile up to the moon."

Stanley stayed quiet while Amato was ranting. If all of this was true, Amato had a reason to be angry. What wasn't clear was whether Cooper had purposely cut corners or had just made an honest mistake.

"Did he know he was supposed to rinse the dishes first?" Stanley asked.

"Of course! I showed him the big sprayer. Who would put chunky dishes into a machine? Who would do this?"

"Did you show him how to rinse the dishes?" Stanley asked. "He's fifteen. It's his first job. He doesn't know anything."

Amato shook his head and waggled his index finger. "When I was fifteen," he said, "I was making bread and churning butter. I was killing pigs and chasing down chickens! No one would have to show me how to rinse a plate!"

"It sounds like he made an honest mistake. I think you should give him another chance."

"Listen to me," Amato said. "All anger and petulance aside. I don't need him. He is a good sweeper when he sweeps, but there is very little to sweep. Nathan can sweep up three times a day, no issue. He cleared tables okay, but Nathan is faster. I'm sorry, but he must go away. I thought he could wash dishes, but he turned them into meatloaf."

****

Later that evening, Stanley was in the kitchen making chili dogs. He hadn't brought up his talk with Amato, but seeing that Cooper was still on edge, he said, "Just so you know, the dish thing could have happened to anyone. It's not fair that he won't give you another chance."

"So I don't have to go back?" Cooper asked.

"No. We'll find something else for you to do. You want cheese on your chili dog?"

Before Cooper could answer, there was a knock on the door. Stanley wiped his hands on a dish towel and started for the door. Before he could get there, the knock came again, this time louder and in a tight bunch of three. Stanley opened the door and was immediately pushed out of the way by Lillian.

"Out of the way, old man," she said. "Good lord, what are you cooking? Smells like something died and ended up on your plate, only not in a good way."

After scanning the room and finding Cooper seated on the couch, she strode over to him and said, "Well, are you going to sit there all night, or are you going to stand up and introduce yourself? Been here for a hundred years and you still haven't introduced yourself."

Cooper looked to Stanley. His eyes had a confused, pleading quality, that made Stanley shrug his shoulders in response. Cooper stood up, but before he could say anything, Lillian said, "Cooper! You think I don't know who you are? Silly boy. Now give me a hug."

Cooper stood completely still.

"Come on," she said. "Bring it in." Cooper did as he was told. Lillian squeezed him tight for half a second before abruptly letting go of him and letting him fall back on the couch.

She turned to Stanley. "What are we eating?" she demanded.

Stanley laughed. This was why he loved her. She had a way of coming into a room like a wrecking ball. She had no filter, no care about what people thought about her. If she offended you, that was your problem. There was no guessing with Lillian. If something bothered her, you knew about it. He could tell that she'd had a drink or two before coming over which tended to bring out these qualities even more. Stanley scratched his head and motioned to the hot dogs on the counter knowing she would disapprove.

"Good lord!" Lillian said, turning back to Cooper. "This

is how he feeds you? You have any idea what's in those things?"

Cooper shook his head.

"Yeah, well, nobody else does, either. No wonder you're grouchy! All right, Stanley, put on a better looking shirt. You're taking me to dinner and a movie. I don't know what's playing, but it's got to be better than this horror show."

Cooper laughed.

"I don't know why you're laughing," Lillian said. "You're going, too. Hop up. Might want to run a comb through that hair. Stanley! Where's the wine? I want a drink before we go."

"You know exactly where it is," Stanley said. "You're the only one who drinks it."

"Of course I know where it is. That was code for, 'Get your lady friend a glass of wine.' Cooper! You like old movies? Probably never seen one. No superheroes tonight. Just good old fashioned overacting."

Stanley poured her a glass of wine and then he and Cooper disappeared into the bedroom to change and get cleaned up. When they reappeared, they stood in front of Lillian as if for a uniform check in the military. Lillian drank the rest of her wine in one swallow and said, "Why are you looking at me like that? I don't care what you wear. Let's go. We'll pick up shrimp on our way down."

"Don't forget your purse," Stanley said.

"Why would I bring my purse? You're paying."

Shrimp, of course, was Ned, and he was just as confused and overwhelmed as Stanley and Cooper had been when he opened the door and Lillian started giving him similar instructions. He got it worse, though, because he didn't have any wine. Lillian didn't get drunk, exactly. What alcohol did, more than anything, was enhance her personality. The fact that she tended to be loud and bossy to begin with, made those occasions when she decided to have a few drinks interesting to say the least.

Ned changed out of his bathrobe and into a simple red shirt and plaid golf shorts. Stanley was surprised that Lillian hadn't harassed him about being in his bathrobe at five o'clock in the evening.

"Well," Ned said. "Does this suit mother hen?" Ned had been calling her that for as long as he could remember. Lillian apparently didn't mind, because she never said anything about it. She didn't say anything this time, either. What she did say was, "Don't you have something with stripes? It would make you look taller."

As they made their way down the Aspen wing to the restaurant, Lillian looped one arm through Cooper's arm and the other one through Stanley's. Cooper had been doing his best to trail behind them, but Lillian made it clear that she would drag him if need be. Ned purposely hung back. Stanley didn't blame him. When Lillian was in this kind of mood, she tended to be hard on Ned.

Before they got to the entrance of the restaurant, Cooper abruptly stopped. "I don't want to go in," he said.

"What are you talking about?" Lillian said.

"He got fired today," Stanley said, and he felt a guilty twinge that he hadn't brought it up sooner. It was like they were dragging him back into the lion's den.

"First of all, you can't fire a volunteer, so stop it. Second of all, I know all about it. That's partly why we're going. The other reason is that I'm starving and I have no food in my room and all you have is hot dogs and something masquerading as chili." Lillian turned to Cooper. "You have two choices in life: You can run and hide or you can meet things head on."

Cooper didn't budge.

"Well, you can't go the next two and a half months without eating," Lillian said. "And if you eat nothing but what Stanley feeds you, you'll be dead long before then. So this is what you do: If Amato makes an appearance, you look him dead in the face and give him your best smile. Believe me, that'll unnerve him more than anything. You can't live your life avoiding things that are unpleasant. Okay?"

Cooper looked to Stanley.

"If he gives you a hard time," Stanley said, "We'll leave."

"No," Lillian said. "If he gives you a hard time, I'll give him a hard time right back."

"What are we talking about?" Ned said

"Jesus you need to get your ears checked," Lillian said.

"Cooper accidentally ruined Amato's dishes, so Amato fired him," Stanley said.

"How do you ruin dishes?"

"It doesn't matter," Lillian said. "Amato was looking for a reason to get rid of him and he found one."

Cooper finally agreed and they entered the restaurant. As they were being seated, Nathan walked by and patted him on the shoulder but didn't say anything.

"See," Lillian said. "Nathan understands. He didn't even have to say anything. Good kid."

"This is the way I see it," Ned said. "If he broke the dishes—"

"He didn't break the dishes," Stanley said.

"How do you ruin a dish without breaking it?"

"Never mind," Stanley said.

Tracey came over and took their order. She squeezed Cooper's arm and whispered, "It could have happened to anyone," before turning to the rest of the table and asking if they were ready to order.

"Wine," Lillian said, "all the way around. And I'll have the baked chicken with green beans."

"All the way around?" Tracey asked.

Lillian motioned for Tracey to come close. She whispered in her ear: "Don't worry. I'll drink the kid's wine. I just want him to feel included." Tracey nodded and turned around, but Lillian caught her by her shirt and added, "Keep em' coming."

"I'll have coffee and a hamburger with fries," Ned said.

"Me, too," Stanley said. "Cooper, you want a hamburger?"

Cooper nodded.

"Make it three burgers and fries."

"Coffee?" Lillian said, looking between Stanley and Ned. "No, no, they'll have wine." Lillian suddenly threw her hands in the air and said, "We're all drinking wine!" The other diners turned and stared, but quickly turned back around when they saw who it was. "That's right," Lillian said. "Go back to your eggnog and biscuits," which was a strange thing to say, even for her.

Amato didn't make an appearance until Tracey was bringing out the food. She was halfway to their table when Amato suddenly called to her from the kitchen and ordered her back. After a few minutes, she returned with their food. When she set Cooper's hamburger down in front of him it was on a paper plate and she quickly switched out his regular utensils with plastic ones. "Sorry," she said, rolling her eyes. "Chef's orders."

"Oh, geez," Cooper said.

Lillian laughed and shook her head. Stanley tried to hold it in, but he laughed, too. Ned said, "I don't get it."

A moment later, Amato sprung from the kitchen door holding a regular plate and utensils over his head and brought them over. "Give me that!" he said, snatching Cooper's hamburger. "I trust you to eat off of plates, just no wash them! There you go! Now you eat like an animal! Growing boy. Good boy, perhaps, but hard to tell. Good sweeper, just not so good at more technical things."

"If he's a good sweeper, you should give him his job back," Lillian said.

Amato shook his head. "Perhaps, but perhaps no. I can't be replacing dishes every other day. Besides, Nathan can handle everything, sweeping, too, so he will not be needed, but I did have a chat with our little she-devil in the fitness room, and she was complaining about all the weights being scattered all over the place and the mirrors being smudged, and I say to her, 'I'll bet the floor could use a good sweeping, too!' and she says yes and I say I know just the boy for the job. See her tomorrow, bright and early! And don't worry, there are no dishes in the fitness room!" And with that, he banged his hand on the table and returned to the kitchen.

"See there," Lillian said. "Problem solved."

She said it like what had just happened was the most normal thing in the world, but the truth was that they were all surprised, most of all Cooper, who sat in a sort of stunned silence.

"Well, Cooper," Stanley said, patting his knee. "Looks like you got yourself another job."

"What if I don't want it?" Cooper asked.

"That's the definition of a job," Ned said. "Show me a job someone wants and what you have isn't a job."

"Don't listen to him," Lillian said. "It's got to beat sweeping up food. You'll like Kelly, too. She's cute. She's tough, but she'll treat you fair."

Cooper didn't look convinced.

"You know how you go through life without getting yelled at?" Lillian said. "You do a good job. She tells you to clean the mirrors, you clean the mirrors. Take a little pride in it. It'll go a long way."

"Look at this," Ned said, sitting back and smiling. "Lillian has a soft, insightful side. And here I thought she was just loud."

"It doesn't work," Lillian said.

"What?" Ned asked.

"That shirt. You look shorter than ever."

"Well, looks like we need to catch the early show tonight so Cooper can get a good night sleep for his big day tomorrow," Stanley said.

Cooper groaned.

"Don't let Kelly catch you loafing," Ned said. "She threw one of those resistance band things at me once for standing around when I should have been working out."

"Don't listen to him, you'll be fine," Stanley said. "Just do what she tells you. She doesn't smile much, or laugh, or compliment people, so don't get offended if she doesn't shower you with praise." Stanley decided to stop talking about it. It seemed like all he was doing was making Cooper more nervous.

They were halfway through their food when Marie Chord walked in. After looking around for a moment, she chose a table close to the kitchen. As she walked by their table, Ned touched her arm and asked, "How's that cat doing, Marie?" Marie stopped and looked down at his hand but didn't remove it. "I'm not sure," she said. "He hasn't said anything yet." Ned laughed, perhaps a little too loudly, which made her flush.

When Marie was safely out of hearing range, Lillian leaned across the table. "Well, well, what do we have here?" she said. "Marie Chord trying to move in on my little Ned?"

"Looks like Ned's trying to move in on her," Stanley said.

Ned turned to Stanley. "Really? You're taking her side on this? Well, I'll have you know that I find her interesting. She's a writer, you know?"

"About cats, apparently," Lillian said, adding, "Well, I think it's adorable!"

Cooper laughed despite obviously not wanting to.

"I've got an idea," Lillian said. "Marie! We're all going to a movie after dinner. Why don't you join us?"

Marie and everyone else in the restaurant heard her, including Amato, who poked his head out of the kitchen and said, "Please, loud woman! You are turning my restaurant into a rough house! Please!"

Lillian rolled her eyes. "So what do you say, Marie?"

"I suppose I could," Marie said.

"Great, we'll save you a seat next to Ned," Lillian said.

Ned looked apologetically at Marie, and then turned to Stanley.

"Don't look at me," Stanley said. "You were the one that was afraid to ask her."

"What? I asked her about the cat, didn't I?" Ned said.

"Let this be a lesson, Cooper," Lillian said. "If you want something, come right out and ask for it. Don't waste a bunch of time talking about cats."

****

The movie showing that evening was the 1997 classic As Good as it Gets, starring Jack Nicholson, Helen Hunt and Greg Kinnear. They barely made it on time because Ned refused to go in without first getting a large popcorn for himself, and then, as an afterthought, a small popcorn for Marie, who swore she didn't want it, but ended up taking it anyway and holding it without eating it for the entire movie. The Last Stop Theater didn't show new releases, only those movies deemed worthy of inclusion in the movie library through various polls taken over the years. As Good as it Gets was one of Stanley and Lillian's favorites. While Marie had never had the pleasure of seeing it, Ned had seen it several times, too, and knew most of the lines by heart. That's why Stanley bopped Ned on the back of the head when he asked him for the seventh time if Jack Nicholson's character and Helen Hunt's character eventually got together. He got smacked again at the end of the movie when he started sniffling and blew his nose when the two characters kissed, except this time it was Lillian who reached over Stanley and Cooper to get a whack at him.

Stanley wasn't sure how Cooper would react to the movie. It wasn't exactly a movie for teenagers, but Stanley caught him laughing a couple of times, especially during the restaurant scenes, and he couldn't help smiling to himself. Sharing a great movie with someone who has never seen it was one of life's simple pleasures.

"I just loved that movie," Marie said, as they were walking out. "I could watch it again and again. If only I could write something that good! The dialog is just brilliant."

They were all in the middle of agreeing when Ned suddenly ran out in front of Lillian and Marie and dropped down on one knee. "You make me want to be a better man!" he said in his best Jack Nicholson voice, which actually wasn't that bad.

"Yeah, well, you make me want to drown myself," Lillian said.

"Fine by me," Ned said, standing up. "I wasn't talking to you anyway."

"Now children," Stanley said.

Lillian threw her arm around Ned. "You are a good man, Ned," she said, which was her way of apologizing for the drowning comment, which had been rude, even for her.

"Thank you," Ned said. "And you're not nearly as mean as you look."

As they approached the Buena Vista wing, Lillian said, "Well, this is where I leave you. Stanley, if you had more wine I'd probably stay over, but you don't and I do, so I bid you all farewell. Good luck tomorrow, Cooper. You'll do great."

"Thanks," Cooper said.

"Good night, Marie. Glad you could join us . . . On second thought, you come with me. After all this manliness, I think we need a nightcap. I've got three bottles of wine in my room with our name on it."

Marie tried to come up with an excuse, but once Lillian had her mind set on something, there was no getting out of it.

"Well, I guess that would be okay," Marie said, and

Lillian took her by the arm and off they went. They were already giggling.

"Marie won't be getting any writing done tomorrow," Ned said.

"She'll be lucky if she gets out of bed tomorrow," Stanley said. It was going to be a long, strange evening for Marie, and it made all three of them laugh.

Ned peeled off down the Western wing, waving his hand over his head and saying, "Good night, gentlemen," and Stanley and Cooper continued on to Stanley's room. When they got there, Stanley asked him, "Did you have a good time tonight?"

Cooper thought for a minute. "Yeah," he said, "it was sort of fun," and that was good enough for Stanley.

CHAPTER TEN

Kelly was in a good mood. Some would say this was as rare as a total eclipse of the sun, but she had a good reason to be. She had gotten word that Chris, her live in boyfriend going on seven years now, was planning on proposing to her. One of his friends had slipped up after a night of heavy drinking and mentioned something about a ring. A similar thing had happened in the past, but it had turned out that Chris was getting her a replica Super Bowl ring for her birthday. He meant well. This time the ring was real. She hadn't let Chris's hungover friend leave until he confirmed it. What wasn't clear was when Chris was planning on proposing. It had taken him almost seven years to get this far, so there was no telling, but at least he was planning. Chris was a professional bodybuilder and kickboxer. His nickname was The Green Giant because of his enormous stature and the green shorts and tank top he always wore. His gentle nature, despite his chosen profession, and his uncanny habit of making her laugh at the most ridiculous things, made it impossible for her to picture herself with anyone else.

She found Cooper just inside the entrance, looking around, shifting his weight from one foot to the other. Amato had told her all about him, describing him as "a slovenly little creature with a talent for sweeping but who lacked focus." Kelly was expecting the stereotypical difficult teenager; one with a smirk and a smart comment for anyone over the age of sixteen. In a way, she had been looking forward to it. Kelly had a talent for wiping smirks off of faces. But it was not to be. When she saw Cooper, she was both happy and disappointed. He looked like other boys his age, but he didn't strike her as particularly difficult. It looked to her like he was trying his best to look calm and cool while obviously being scared to death.

"Cooper, right?" Kelly said, holding out her hand.

Cooper looked at her hand but didn't take it.

"What's the matter, never shake hands with a woman?"

Cooper didn't say anything.

"Little small, aren't ya?" Kelly said, squeezing his arm.

"I guess so," Cooper said..

"Well, you guessed right. We'll fix that."

"I've always been short," Cooper said.

"Can't do anything about that, but we can bulk up everything else."

"I'm supposed to work," Cooper said, "not exercise."

"I know, but that'll change. Amato says you sweep pretty good," she said, rolling her eyes.

"I guess," Cooper said, "but he didn't like the way I did the dishes."

"Well, Amato thinks that anything done by anyone but himself is done wrong. The only reason he lets Nathan do anything, is it gives him someone to yell at. Did he feed you?"

"What?"

"Did he feed you? You know, like food?"

"He made me a sandwich."

"He likes you. That's how you know with Amato. He

would never waste food on someone he doesn't like."

"He has a funny way of showing it," Cooper said.

"That he does. Don't worry. He hardly ever comes in here . . . Okay, hand it over . . ."

"What?" Cooper said.

"Your phone. You kids don't leave home without it. I can't have you staring at your phone all day."

"My grandpa wouldn't let me bring it," Cooper said. "He said it was for my own safety."

Kelly smiled. "Good man. All right, let's get started. Follow me . . . This is the cardio area. You see those ladies over there?"

Cooper nodded.

"Steer clear. They're ornery. By the way, you might want to get your hair out of your eyes. There are all kinds of things to trip on and bop your head on if you're not careful . . . Not much to do in here but the glass. Sometimes the exercise bikes get moved around. If that's the case, put them back in a neat row like they are now. I like things clean, just so you know. See that closet over there by the treadmills? The Windex and rags are in there. There's also a small ladder so you can get up top. If you're ever here late, I'll have you wipe down all the machines. The disinfectant is in there, too."

"You want me to wash the windows?" Cooper asked.

"Would you want to spend an hour looking out a dirty window? It's hard enough to get some of them in here."

"How do you clean them?" Cooper asked.

Kelly studied him for a minute to make sure he was serious.

"Sorry," she said. "I keep forgetting you've never had a job before."

"I know it's stupid, but I don't want to get yelled at anymore."

"I don't blame you. Here's a secret for you, and don't go spreading this around or I'll kill you in your sleep. I'm not nearly as angry and violent as people make me out to be. I can go overboard sometimes, but I mostly do it because it's fun."

"It's fun to yell at people?" Cooper asked.

"Yeah, sort of. Besides, at this point everyone expects it. If I was suddenly all warm and cuddly they'd think I was sick. Anyway, I'm not planning on yelling at you or throwing things at you—"

"You throw things?"

"Sure. I don't usually hurt people, though. My point is that if you do a good job, you don't have to worry about any of that stuff."

Kelly spent the next several minutes showing him the fine art of cleaning glass. When she was done, she gave him the rag and glass cleaner and had him do it himself.

"There," she said. "Easy enough, right?"

"Sure."

"Do the mirrors the same way," she said, pointing at the mirrors that lined the far wall. "Once they're clean, I want you spot-cleaning them throughout the day. If you catch one of the oldsters smudging them up, give them a good swat with the rag."

Cooper laughed.

"I'm not kidding," Kelly said.

"Should I start cleaning them now?"

"No, I'm going to show you everything first. Then I'll test you on it. If you pass, then you can start . . . I'm kidding, Cooper. Let's go."

As they picked their way out of the cardio area, they heard one of the two ornery ladies remark that he'd be cute if only he'd get a haircut.

"That's the truth," Kelly said, turning to him. "Just so you know."

"Thanks," Cooper said. His face was flushed. Kelly laughed.

"Okay, this is the general weight room. This is the

trouble spot. You see this? Already there's weight plates lying around. These are weight trees. This is what the weight plates go on. They're marked. See there, five, ten, twenty-five? Make sure the tens go with the tens and the fives go with the fives, etc.. Understand? You might also find resistance bands lying around. If you do, they go on the wall over there."

"Old people lift weights?" Cooper asked.

"Why shouldn't they lift weights?"

"I don't know. I just thought—"

"Yeah, well, that's what everyone thinks," Kelly said. "But here's the thing: Strong people live longer." What she usually said was, "Strong people are harder to kill," but Cooper was already on edge, so she decided to tone it down.

Cooper nodded.

"So, the moral of the story is if you see weights lying around, put them back where they go. Just make sure no one is using them. If you're not sure, ask around. Over there is the dumbbell rack. Same thing applies. They need to be in order. The top tier goes from three pounds to twenty-five pounds. The bottom tier goes from thirty to fifty."

"Fifty pounds?" Cooper said.

"Only a handful of the men ever use those, but if they're out of the rack, you can roll them to where they go," she said. "Here, I'll show you."

Kelly took one of the fifty-pound dumbbells out of the rack and set it on the floor and rolled it with her foot. "When you get it to where it goes, flip it up like this . . ." Kelly tipped the dumbbell so it rested on its top, "and then grab it around the handle with both hands, like this . . . And then bend at the knees . . . And then heave it into place like this. Now you try . . ."

Cooper did as he was told and was pleasantly surprised when the dumbbell came off the ground with relative ease and he was able to maneuver it into place without too much trouble.

"See there," Kelly said. "Not too bad when you know what you're doing."

"For sure," Cooper said, and Kelly, surprised at hearing something other than 'I guess,' said, "Well, that's better. Confidence! I like it."

Cooper saw one of the fifteens between the twenty-fives and quickly put it back in its place.

Kelly nodded. "All this goes for the plate-loaded machines, too."

It was obvious that Cooper wasn't quite sure what she was talking about, so she took him over to a Hammer-Strength Inclined Chest Press and showed how the plates slid onto the arms in back. "If you see weights on them and no one is using them, go ahead and unload it . . . There's one over there."

Cooper made the mistake of trying to slide one of the twenty-five pound plates off with one hand, nearly dropping it on his toe.

"Careful," Kelly said. "You're not allowed to get hurt . . .Okay, over here is the refrigerator where we keep the bottled water. Nothing exciting here, just make sure it's stocked at all times."

"Do they have to pay for it?"

"Nope. Everything is free. There are cases of water in the closet by the bathrooms . . . Which brings me to the bathrooms. This is where I can be a bit of a stickler. There is nothing worse than walking into a filthy bathroom. So, I want you checking them every hour. Don't worry, most of the people that use them learned how to aim and flush a long time ago, so they never get too bad, but make sure there aren't any paper towels on the floor. If the trash is getting full, take it out. Make sure the mirrors and sinks are clean. Keep the paper towels and toilet paper stocked. There's more in the closet where the water is."

She could see Cooper getting overwhelmed. "Follow me," she said. "I'll show you where everything is."

For the next fifteen minutes, she showed him how to change out the paper towels and toilet paper, showed him how to clean the sinks and where and how to change the mop water. "This is my pet peeve," she said, pointing at the mop bucket. "The only thing that drives me crazier than a mop bucket filled with dirty water is someone mopping with dirty mop water, so change it often."

Cooper smiled and nodded.

"I'm serious," she said. "Don't make me hurt you."

Kelly suddenly turned and yelled, "Don't let me catch you using the baby weights, Roger!" She turned and winked at Cooper. Roger shook his head and re-racked the fifteen-pound dumbbells and grabbed the twenty-fives. "Wouldn't think of it," Roger said.

"Okay," Kelly said, turning back to Cooper. "So, for today, start with the bathrooms. When you're done with that, come get me and I'll check them. That way if you missed something, you can fix it right then and there and I don't have to find it later and scream at you. When that's done, start on the glass and keep an eye out for loose weights. Got it?"

Cooper nodded.

"I'll be around if you need me. You should be able to hear me." Kelly squeezed his arm and told him to get to it, which he did.

****

It took Cooper almost a half-hour to clean the mens bathroom. He knew it was probably taking longer than it should, but he was trying to do a good job. He had a near catastrophe when he accidentally tipped over the mop bucket and barely caught the water before it seeped out the door and into the hallway. The good part was that the floor was extra clean. When he thought he was done, he got Kelly to check it.

"Well, I see we have two different ideas about what is clean and what is not," Kelly said after looking around. "No streaks, Cooper, and get the whole sink, even the outside. Floor looks good, though. Come get me when you're done with the womens bathroom."

"You want me to go in there?" Cooper said.

Kelly laughed. "Looks pretty much like the other bathroom, Cooper. This is what you do," she said, and pounded on the door with both fists. "Anyone in there?" When no one answered, she opened the door and kicked the door stopper down so everyone would know it was being cleaned. "Not a bad idea to do that in the mens room, too," she said. "It'll keep someone from running you over if you're cleaning behind the door."

The womens bathroom took half the time to clean. Women, he guessed, were easier on bathrooms. There was an embarrassing moment when a woman rushed in and said, "You can stay if you want, but the flood gates are opening," and Cooper made a hasty retreat.

At five past noon, Cooper was cleaning the mirrors when he saw Amato in the reflection. He was talking to Kelly. She had a hand on her hip, but she was smiling and nodding. He handed her a paper bag, looked in his general direction, then nodded and left.

Kelly approached Cooper and held out the bag. "This is for you," she said. "You can eat it outside or in the office, up to you. Lunch is a half-hour. Don't be late."

Cooper looked in the bag and found what looked like a tuna fish sandwich wrapped in cellophane and a bag of baked lays potato chips. The sandwich was huge. It looked like it had a whole can of tuna on it. Kelly saw him looking at it. "I told you he liked you," she said. "By the way, Amato said, 'This will get him big and stronger!'" The imitation was good. When she topped it off by flexing both biceps, Cooper laughed.

Cooper decided to eat the sandwich out back. It occurred

to him that if he saw Holy Moses, he might be able to coax him over with a bit of the sandwich. Maybe then Holy would forgive him for the restaurant mishap. Holy wasn't out back, so he went around the other side of the building and found him rolling around in the shade beneath a tree. Cooper decided it would be best to keep his distance, so he stayed where he was. Holy abruptly rolled over, sat up and stared at Cooper. It wasn't an angry stare, but it wasn't particularly welcoming, either. Cooper held up part of the sandwich and weakly patted his knee, but Holy made no indication that he was more than mildly curious. Cooper thought about saying something like, "Want some cheese, boy?" but thought better about it. Holy wasn't likely to be thrilled about being tricked, and he'd already seen what short work Holy could make of him, so he sat down in the grass Indian-style and ate his sandwich and chips. Holy sniffed the air a few times, but eventually rolled over on his back and went to sleep.

After he was done eating, Cooper laid back in the grass and closed his eyes. When he opened them again, he realized, alarmingly, that he had no way of knowing how long he'd been out here. While he was pretty sure he hadn't actually gone to sleep, he had a feeling that he'd been daydreaming for longer than he should have been. He crumpled up the sack and ran back towards the fitness center, tossing the bag in the trash before opening the door and running in. Kelly was busy talking to a group of ladies, and he tried to sneak past her to where his cleaning supplies were.

"When I say a half-hour, that's what I mean, Cooper," she said.

He started to explain, but she had resumed talking to the women.

"Sorry," Cooper said, and the funny thing was that he actually meant it.

The rest of the day went off without a hitch. Kelly was right: for some reason, people were really bad about putting their weights back where they found them, but he didn't mind. It gave him something to do.

At four o'clock, Kelly found him. "Well, what do you think?" she asked. "You want to stick around for a while?"

"Sure!" Cooper said, and she was surprised by the enthusiasm in his voice.

"Great. You can knock off for the day. I'll take it from here. You did good today."

"Thanks," Cooper said.

"Seven o'clock tomorrow. It shouldn't take you as long to clean the bathrooms now that you know what you're doing."

Cooper said he would be there and turned to leave.

"Oh, and Cooper?" Kelly said. "Buy a watch. Or steal one."

Chapter Eleven

Stanley noticed a change in Cooper that evening. He had grown used to Cooper spending the majority of time sitting in silence, staring at his phone, so he was surprised when Cooper walked in and joined him and Ned at the dining room table. They were in the middle of a not-so-friendly game of chess.

"There he is," Stanley said. "So how did it go?"

"Good," Cooper said. Stanley, denied the usual aloofness, looked up at him to make sure he wasn't being sarcastic.

"Really? Kelly wasn't too hard on you then?"

"She's actually kind of nice."

Stanley raised his eyebrows. Nice? He could count on one hand the number of times that word had been used to describe Kelly.

"I wouldn't get too excited," Ned said. "There's probably a law against being mean to young people."

Stanley rolled his eyes, partly because of what Ned had said, but also because Ned had been staring at one of Stanley's pawns since before Cooper had come in and he appeared no closer to making a move.

"Good lord, would you move already?" Stanley said.

"Can you keep it down please?" Ned said. "I'm trying to concentrate."

Stanley turned to Cooper. "What did you do for lunch? You could have come back here and I could have made you something."

"Amato brought me a sack lunch," Cooper said.

"Really?" Stanley said, arching his eyebrows for the second time. "Well, what do you know about that?"

Ned apparently decided that if Stanley wanted to trade pawns, he was going to have to initiate the aggression because he moved his knight in front of his king. Stanley glanced at the board and quickly took Ned's pawn. Ned sighed and went back to studying the board.

"You should probably take my pawn," Stanley said. "You know, even things up."

"Not so fast. I'm just making sure you're not setting me up for something."

"We're four moves in, Ned. Good grief." His exasperation was mostly fake. Stanley had been playing chess with Ned for a long time and had grown accustomed to his maddening style of play.

"You okay?" Stanley said. Cooper had moved over to the couch and was lying down. A fifteen-year-old kid sleeping at five o'clock in the afternoon was usually a sign that something was wrong.

Cooper nodded and shut his eyes.

"Would you take my pawn already," Stanley said, turning back to Ned. "We're both growing older here."

Cooper suddenly sat up and asked, "Do you have a watch I can borrow?"

Ned snorted. "I wouldn't trust any watch your granddad gives you."

Stanley glanced down at his dead watch. He still hadn't gotten around to getting it fixed.

Stanley started to tell Cooper that he was all out of watches, but Ned interrupted him. "Here, take this one," he said. "What do I need to know the time for?" Ned unclipped his watch, slipped it off his wrist and tossed it to Cooper. It was big and gold with a thick band and a scratched face. Cooper put it on, but it flopped around on his wrist.

"No thanks," Cooper said.

"No thanks? You need a watch, don't you?" Ned said.

"It doesn't fit."

"So put it in your pocket."

"What do you need a watch for?" Stanley asked.

"I was late getting back from lunch because I lost track of time."

"Not smart, kid," Ned said. "You lose this gig and they'll kick you to the curb. Nothing your old granddad can do about it, either."

"Oh, stop," Stanley told Ned. "You're just mad at the horse."

"Horse?" Cooper said, sitting up.

"Well," Stanley said. "We were going to surprise you later, but we might as well tell you. We got a horse today."

"Who?"

"Us. Everyone. The whole community. He's down in the barn." Stanley paused and looked at Ned. "And it's not just any horse. It's THE horse."

Ned snorted and took Stanley's pawn and tossed it next to the board.

Stanley laughed, remembering the story Ned had told him that morning.

****

Ned had been sitting on the front porch swing drinking a cup of coffee when a truck pulling a horse trailer pulled up. He liked to come out sometimes in the early morning when the air was still cool. Lots of folks visited loved ones on their way up to the mountains, so it wasn't uncommon to find trucks with boats or campers parked in the parking lot. But when the truck bypassed the parking lot and pulled into the roundabout and parked, Ned took notice. And when the horse stuck his head out the side window to see what was going on, Ned couldn't help feeling an odd sense of déjà vu.

A moment later, the lobby doors opened and Beverly, followed by Harry and a couple of the admin women, AKA the chin wags, came out to meet the driver. This was something new. This obviously wasn't just any visitor because all of them seemed excited. There had been talk over the years about getting a horse to go with the horse barn down on the northern tip of the property, but it had always been just talk. The barn had been there before the facility went up, and had mostly gone unused except for overflow from Harry's maintenance shed.

Ned watched as a man in his mid-fifties and wearing boots and a hat popped out of the truck and went around the side and patted the horse on his head. Beverly and the others joined him, all admiring the horse, who seemed to be enjoying all the attention.

"Well, here he is. He's a great horse, loves attention," the man was telling them. "Loved to race, too, just didn't care for winning!"

They all laughed.

"One time," the man continued, "he stopped dead in the middle of a race and jumped the rail to go investigate a family of rabbits. The jockey was unable to coax him back on the track until he had satisfied his curiosity. Crazy horse. I guess you all know what happened in his last race. Never seen anything like it. Hell, I've never even heard of anything like it."

Ned had gotten up and was approaching the group when the man opened the back of the trailer and took the horse by the reins. "He can be stubborn, but if you keep a bag of M&M's on you, he'll go to the ends of the earth for you," the man said and Ned dropped his coffee.

"How is this possible?" Ned asked, ignoring his spilled coffee. He was looking at Harry when he said it, but the question was really directed at the racing gods. "It's not enough he costs me a fortune? Now I have to look at him every day?"

Ain't He Something walked out of the trailer and went to investigate Ned's spilled coffee.

"He's one good looking racehorse," the man was saying. "You guys are lucky to have him. It'll be nice for him to live out his days . . . Well, retired!" The man laughed, apparently at the idea of a retirement home for racehorses.

Ned tugged at Harry's shirt and asked him what was going on, but Harry flicked his hand away and ignored him.

Beverly said, "What do you think is going on, Ned? We finally got a horse. We've been on the adoption list forever, but there was never one that was quite right until this one came along. He's got one heck of a story. Ms. Hathaway told us about him. He stopped right in the middle of the race to eat M&M's—"

"I know!" Ned said. "I was right there. This horse cost me a fortune!"

"Cost the owner a fortune, too," the man said. "A racehorse with no interest in winning races is too expensive to keep. Between boarding fees and training fees and vet bills and the cost just to feed the bugger, well, it was too much. Glad he's coming here. He's a real friendly horse."

Ned shook his head. "Unbelievable."

"His name is *Ain't He Something*—"

"I know!" Ned snapped. "He was ahead by ten lengths! I would have been rich."

As if on cue, *Ain't He Something* sidestepped everyone and approached Ned.

"What do you want?" Ned said.

Ain't He Something nuzzled Ned's shirt.

"I don't have anything," Ned said, disgusted, and turned

and went inside to tell Stanley about his misfortune.

Stanley was skeptical of Ned's story until Lillian showed up at the door and asked, "Have you seen the freaking racehorse?"

****

"So it's really him?" Cooper asked.

"Yes, it's him," Ned said. "Now can we drop it?"

"Can I go see him?"

"I'd wait until the morning. Let him settle in a little bit. It's probably a big change for him. Tomorrow's Saturday. You can spend the whole day with him if you like—Ned, move already!"

"It's your move, wise guy. Personally, I don't want anything to do with that horse. He's bad luck. If I get near him, I'll probably get struck by lightning. What time is it?"

"How would I know?" Stanley said.

"Cooper, what time is it?"

Cooper dug Ned's watch out of his pocket.

"Four-forty," Cooper said.

"I have to go," Ned said, standing up.

"What? We're in the middle of a game here," Stanley said.

"So leave the board how it is and we'll finish tomorrow. I'm making dinner for someone."

"Really?" Stanley said. "For who?"

Ned hesitated. "Marie Chord."

"You're kidding? Marie Chord is going to let you cook for her?"

"Sure . . . Certainly, I mean."

Stanley coughed.

"Cough all you want," Ned said. "Marie happens to think I'm adorable."

"She told you this?"

"Well, no, but I saw it in her face."

"Maybe she's just hungry and doesn't have any food," Cooper said from the couch.

"That is an excellent point," Stanley said.

"You know, Cooper," Ned said, heading for the door. "I liked you better when you didn't talk."

Chapter Twelve

There were few things Harry enjoyed more than watering. Something about it made everything seem right with the world. It was his favorite time of the day. After his morning trash patrol, he loaded up his hoses in his wheelbarrow and set about watering the hundred-or-so plants, pots, flowers, and bushes around the property. If he was left alone, he could manage it in a couple of hours. When he upgraded the sprinkler system, he'd added lines that ran to the various flower beds and drip lines to the gardens, but they were only scheduled to run on the days when he wasn't there to water them. There were mornings when he had to rely on the sprinkler system to do the bulk of the watering, but they were few and far between. The truth was that gardening and tending to his flowers was a kind of therapy. He even talked to them sometimes, albeit under his breath and when no one was around.

Most mornings, Holy Moses joined him, alternating between lying next to where Harry was watering so he could get misted and grabbing hold of the hose to see if he could instigate a game of tug-of-war, but this morning he was nowhere to be found.

If Holy was going to join him, he was going to have to hurry. Ever since *Ain't He Something*'s arrival, his workload had drastically increased. He'd liked the idea of having a horse as much as anyone, but he was quickly finding out that the responsibilities of owning a horse were falling largely on his shoulders. He wasn't really complaining, though. If he'd have known they were seriously considering getting a horse, he would have been better prepared. Now that *Ain't He Something* was here, he had to scramble to mend the fence around the small pasture and fix the barn's leaking roof and loose siding. He was also going to have to figure out a place to store the hay so it wouldn't get wet. But once those things were done, all he had to worry about was feeding him, cleaning out his stall, and making sure he was getting enough exercise, none of which he minded doing, though he wouldn't turn down help if it showed up. The truth was that *Ain't He Something* was proving to be an easy horse to take care of. He was used to a lot of human interaction from his time at the racetrack, and he seemed to genuinely enjoy being around people, which was good, considering all the attention he was going to get from the residents.

Harry finished watering everything that needed immediate attention and headed down to the barn. He'd have to go back around and finish the watering later when he had more time. He wasn't too worried about it. The forecast called for rain later that afternoon. The first thing he noticed when he got down to the barn was that *Ain't He Something* wasn't in it. Nor was he in the pasture. Nor was he anywhere in the immediate area. There weren't any signs that he had broken out of his stall. The door was open, but the latch was still attached to it. It looked like someone had simply let him out. It was probably more likely that *Ain't He Something* had figured out how to let himself out. He was a quirky horse, that was for sure. He'd have to see what he could do about fixing the latch so it was harder to open. But first, he had to find *Ain't He Something*. While having a racehorse loose on the property was definitely cause for concern, Harry wasn't one to panic. He had one simple motto that he lived by: "There's nothing to worry about until there's something to worry about."

On his way out of the barn, Harry ran headlong into a teenage boy. Harry was much bigger than him and sent him flailing. The kid almost went down but caught himself at the last second. Once Harry got a closer look at him, he vaguely recognized him. He'd seen him around. The kid never seemed to say much. Harry didn't hold it against him. Harry had spent his entire life not saying much and he had turned out just fine. He knew that the kid was doing some sort of volunteer work, probably for school, and that he was the grandson of one of the residents, but he didn't know much beyond that.

"You all right?" Harry asked him. "Didn't see you there."

"I came down to see the horse," the kid said, looking over Harry's shoulder at the empty stall. "I thought there was a horse."

"There is a horse," Harry said, looking around. "Somewhere."

"You lost him?"

"Temporarily. What's your name?"

"Cooper."

"So you like horses, Cooper?"

"Yeah."

"Well, I suppose two sets of eyes are better than one. You want to help me find him?"

"Sure."

Harry didn't think *Ain't He Something* was up around any of the main buildings. If he was, he should have come across him while he was watering. You'd think a horse would be a hard thing to miss, but Harry tended to get tunnel vision when he was watering, so he thought they should at least do a quick search around the facilities.

Harry turned around and looked down towards the river. Cooper followed his gaze and asked, "You think he went down there?"

"Hope not. If he takes the path, he'll eventually end up in Colorado Springs. Tell you what, let's go up to the shed and get the golf cart. We'll do a quick tour around the grounds and if we can't find him, we'll head down towards the river. "

Harry was thinking about letting Cooper drive the golf cart but decided against it. It was easy enough to drive, but he already had one potential liability on his hands and he didn't need another one.

Harry figured the easiest way to get an overview of the property was to drive along the mile-long fitness loop. It was a paved path that circled the property. It meandered through the acreage, providing walkers with various hills and stopping points where they could enjoy the scenery. It would give them a good look at every nook and cranny around the buildings, as well as a birds-eye view of the surrounding land. As they started down the path, they passed a small group of walkers. Harry asked them if they'd seen a horse. For some reason, they thought this was funny until they realized he was serious. They assured him that they had not and that they'd keep their eyes open, and Harry and Cooper continued on. Harry whistled a few times, but felt silly and stopped. Holy Moses wouldn't even come to a whistle. He thought about nickering, but he didn't think he could pull it off.

As they rounded the corner by the picnic area, dipped down a hill and were coming up the other side, they heard a commotion from behind them. There was quite a bit of yelling, and one woman shrieked, "Look out!" A moment later, they heard the unmistakable sound of pounding hooves. Seconds later, they watched *Ain't He Something* bank around the corner, dip down the hill and blow by them on the shoulder of the path and disappear over the top of the next hill.

"Holy crow!" Cooper said, and Harry had to agree. It was one thing to watch a racehorse running on a track, but when one passed by two feet in front of you going full speed, "Holy crow!" was as fitting an exclamation as any.

"Well, looks like we found our horse," Harry said.

"He was flying!" Cooper said. "Where do you think he's going?"

"I don't think he's going anywhere," Harry said. "I think that silly horse is running an imaginary race."

This must have struck Cooper as funny because he started giggling. Harry thought about what he had just said and started laughing, too. Hearing the stories of *Ain't He Something*'s antics, he really shouldn't have been surprised. The fitness loop was just about the perfect length for a horse race, and it was a whole lot more interesting to run around than a racing oval.

"He must miss it," Cooper said.

"Racing? I guess so. That's what he did for a long time—sounds like he's coming back around."

Once again, they heard a commotion from the group behind them, though this time it was more laughter than anything, and *Ain't He Something* again appeared around the corner, but this time at a much slower speed. When he was almost to them, he pulled up as if by imaginary reigns and slowed to a trot. He was visibly tired, but he looked happy and alert. For some reason, Harry hadn't thought to bring a lead rope with him. He was used to Holy Moses just following him around, so he hadn't thought to bring one. And speaking of Holy Moses, that revered canine came trotting down the hill in front of them. He'd probably been alerted by the shrieking woman and had come to investigate. His tongue was hanging out and he looked annoyed. Holy stopped and eyeballed all three of them. Judging by the look on his face, he'd been expecting something more interesting.

"Well, look who decided to show up," Harry said. Holy bypassed Cooper and sat down at Harry's feet. *Ain't He Something* leaned his huge head down and sniffed the air around Holy's head. Holy stood up and faced him. Although *Ain't He Something* was many times bigger than him, Holy didn't seem to notice.

"How are we going to get him back to the barn?" Cooper asked, patting *Ain't He Something* on the neck.

Holy did a complete circle around *Ain't He Something* and then laid down.

"That is a really good question," Harry said. "Well, just for the heck of it, let's start heading for the barn and see if he follows."

This worked for a half-dozen steps, but *Ain't He Something* seemed to sense what they were trying to do and came to a halt.

"Come on, boy," Harry said. "Come on, horse!"

Cooper looked sideways at him and Harry laughed. "Well, what else do you call him?"

"I have an idea," Cooper said. "I'll be right back."

Cooper turned and ran back down the path towards the lobby. Harry had no idea what Cooper was doing, but he was open to ideas. It was obvious that *Ain't He Something* wasn't interested in going back to the barn. It appeared that he and Holy Moses had something in common. Holy had a talent for turning himself into an immovable object when pressed to do something he didn't want to do. Harry could only imagine what would happen if *Ain't He Something* used a similar tactic.

The moment Harry saw Cooper returning, he understood. He recalled the man telling them how *Ain't He Something* would follow you anywhere if you had peanut M&M's.

"You know about the M&M's?" Harry asked.

"Yeah, he stole them from me during his last race."

Ain't He Something's ears perked up when Cooper

showed him the bag of M&M's. When *Ain't He Something* tried to take the bag from him, Cooper pulled it away. Holy recognized this as teasing and barked at Cooper. *Ain't He Something* shook his head, snorted, then leaned in and tried again. Holy Moses got up and joined him. While Holy's true love was cheese, he couldn't resist the mysteries of a crinkling wrapper.

Cooper said, "This way," and began walking backwards in the direction of the barn, holding the bag of M&M's out in front of him.

Ain't He Something followed, stretching his neck and head out, occasionally trying to snatch the bag from Cooper. Holy Moses soon lost interest and returned to the golf cart with Harry. There were a few tense moments when *Ain't He Something* stopped and refused to go any further, but the golf cart following behind him and the promise of M&M's proved too great and he carried on to the barn.

When he was back in his stall, happily munching a handful of M&M's, Harry closed the stall door and made sure the latch was secure.

"You're pretty good with him," Harry said.

"He's a neat horse," Cooper said. "I've never even had a dog before."

Judging by Holy's reaction to Cooper, this wasn't surprising. It was obvious that Holy hadn't quite made up his mind about Cooper yet.

"Horses are a lot more work than dogs, I'll tell you that," Harry said.

"I could help," Cooper said, surprising both of them. Harry studied him to make sure he was serious. The truth was that he wouldn't mind the help, but he needed to be able to count on him. If he felt the need to constantly check if things were done right, he'd just as soon do it himself.

"I don't want it to interfere with the other stuff you're doing," Harry said. Judging by the look on Cooper's face, he had suddenly realized that it was likely to do just that.

"I'll have to check with Kelly," Cooper said.

Harry smiled. He'd talk to Kelly himself. If she gave Cooper her endorsement, than he was all right with him. Kelly didn't humor people. If she didn't think Cooper would do a good job, she'd tell him.

"All right, we'll check with Kelly, but in the meantime let's get started on that fence . . ." Harry had been joking about Cooper helping him with the fence, so he was surprised when Cooper smiled and nodded.

"I'm kidding," Harry said. "You don't have to help me."

Cooper looked disappointed. "I want to, though," he said.

"All right," Harry said. "If we're going to get it done before lunch, we best get started . . . After lunch, we'll start on the barn."

Cooper nodded enthusiastically.

"All right, then. I guess you're officially my right-hand man."

CHAPTER THIRTEEN

Cooper made sure to get up early Monday morning so he could get to the fitness center a few minutes early to talk to Kelly. It was easier getting out of bed these days. It helped that he was actually looking forward to the day ahead of him instead of dreading it. He'd spent the weekend working harder than he'd ever worked in his life helping Harry. Between bailing hay, swinging a hammer, and lugging around fence posts, he was exhausted by the time he got back to the room, but it was worth it.

Ain't He Something was a real character. As soon as they had finished mending the fence, he hopped over it with almost no effort at all and began eating the grass on the other side. Harry had taken off his hat and looked at *Ain't He Something* in disbelief. It had occurred to Cooper that the fence might be too low, but he'd decided not to say anything.

After fixing the fence, they'd patched up the barn. Cooper hadn't liked the idea of going way up on a ladder, but Harry talked him through it, and by the end of the day, he was going up and down carrying tools with no problem. Three times that afternoon, *Ain't He Something* wandered off. He always gravitated towards either the courtyard or the lobby. That's where the most people congregated. He was a big hit with both residents and visitors. It wasn't every day you walked out the front door or got out of your car and were greeted by a horse. Harry had spoken to the higher-ups about the issue with the fence and they'd agreed that *Ain't He Something* could roam freely during daylight hours as long as he stayed on the property and no one complained. Staying on the property wasn't going to be a problem. The residents were so generous with snacks that he quickly learned to hang out in high-traffic areas. Most of the time there was a line of residents waiting to feed and pet him. Harry said the novelty of it would eventually wear off, but in the meantime he'd speak to the ladies who wrote the weekly newsletter about putting something in it about limiting the amount they were feeding him. He also told Cooper to keep the M&M's to a minimum.

Cooper entered the fitness center feeling loose and happy. It was only his second day, but he liked being there, though he didn't really know why. It certainly beat the restaurant, he knew that. He preferred the clanking of weights to Amato's shouting any day of the week.

When he entered Kelly's office, he found her leaning over her desk, writing on a desk calendar. Before he could say anything and without looking up, she said, "I changed your hours. Starting tomorrow you'll start at ten and go until six. That should give you enough time to help Harry in the mornings." Harry must have already spoken to Kelly. He was glad. He hadn't been comfortable asking her about it to begin with.

"Thank you," Cooper said. "You don't mind?"

"No, I don't mind. That silly horse has already been by here this morning. I had the door open to let some air in and he poked his head in and looked around before I shooed him out. If I hadn't been here, he probably would have waltzed right in."

"He likes people," Cooper said.

"Yeah, well you tell him to stay outside or me and him are going to have a problem."

"I got a watch," Cooper said, changing the subject. He took Ned's watch out of his pocket and showed it to her.

"That's some watch," she said. "You can keep it in here until lunch if you don't want to carry it around with you. I've got a class to teach in a few minutes, so I won't be around for a while. Don't go thinking you can slack off when I'm not here. I have eyes everywhere." She was smiling, but Cooper didn't take what she said lightly. Kelly grasped him by the shoulders and pointed him towards the door. "Now get out of here before I kick you out. You've got stuff to do."

Cooper was halfway down the hall when Kelly said, "Oh, and Cooper, find me after lunch. I need to talk to you about something."

Cooper had been alive long enough to know that the only thing worse than anticipation was the unknown. Now he had both. He spent the morning speculating on what she wanted to talk to him about, but got nowhere. He was so lost in thought about it that he mopped the womens bathroom floor twice. He was refilling the mop bucket for the third time when he realized what he was doing. By the time he got to the windows and mirrors, the gym was at its peak hours.

He was happy to notice Lillian and Marie on bikes next to each other down towards the end where he was starting. Lillian was wearing some sort of spandex outfit with a matching headband. On anyone else it would have looked silly. Marie was wearing pink sweatpants and a matching sweatshirt, and judging by how much she was sweating, she was regretting it.

"You've got to sweat it out!" Lillian was telling her. "That's the only way."

This was just cryptic enough to make Cooper pause. Lillian saw him and said, "Cooper! How the heck are you?" He hadn't known Lillian for long, and he wondered if she was always this loud. Marie nodded at Cooper and rolled her eyes in Lillian's direction. She looked exhausted, even though she wasn't pedaling very fast.

"Takes us old folks a little longer to get over a hangover," Lillian explained. "Turns out Marie here likes wine a whole lot more than she thought she did. I guess she didn't learn the first time!"

"Wine, Cooper," Marie said. "Never touch it. Or if you do, don't ever drink it with this she-devil."

Lillian laughed. "Don't look at me. The first night was my idea. Last night was all you. Nobody told you to drink the whole bottle."

"Don't listen to her. She tried to kill me," Marie said. " . . . Why are we telling you this? Don't drink, Cooper. Not ever."

"At least not for a few more years," Lillian said.

"And don't ever drink with her," Marie added. "She'll make you drink the whole bottle."

"Okay," Cooper said. "If I drink, I'll do it by myself."

They both laughed.

"Good boy," Lillian said.

When he was done with the mirrors, Cooper went to check for loose weights. There were an unusual number of them lying around and the dumbbell rack was a mess. He had just started reorganizing them when he heard a voice from behind him say, "Don't touch those, kid." The voice belonged to a man with long, gray hair down past his shoulders. He wore red sweatpants and running shoes with no socks, and his shirt was slung over one shoulder, showing off his rippled, hairless body. Veins protruded from his arms and shoulders, and his stomach muscles stuck out.

"Sorry," Cooper said. The man sidestepped Cooper and grabbed the forty pound dumbbells and began lifting them over his head one at a time. When he'd done it eight times on each side, he put them back in the rack and repeated the same thing with the thirty-fives. He repeated this in five pound increments until he got all the way down to the fives.

"Man that burns!" he said when he was done, but he was smiling. "That's called a drop-set, son. That gets them good."

"That looked hard," Cooper said.

"Of course it was hard! Anything worth doing is hard. Look at my hands . . . They're still shaking."

"Why do you do it if it hurts?" Cooper asked.

"No pain, no gain, you ever hear that saying?"

"No," Cooper said.

"Well, you have to shock the muscles if you want them to grow. Right now my muscles are trying to figure out how to deal with what I just put them through. So now they'll get bigger and stronger just in case I put them through that again. See how it works?"

Cooper didn't.

"You take science class in school?"

"Yes," Cooper said.

"Well, if you studied organisms, you learned that they adapt and change in response to stress in their environment. We're the same way. Your body adapts to the stress placed upon it. Now you see?"

"I guess so," Cooper said, but he was having trouble understanding how people were organisms. What he did understand was that this guy didn't look like any other old person he'd ever seen. His grandfather always kept himself trim, and Ned was skinny as a rail, but this guy had muscles like the guys in the magazines he saw at the grocery store.

"Byron talking to you about organisms?" The voice was Kelly's. Cooper turned around and found her standing behind them, her hands on her hips, looking back and forth between them. "I see you two have met. You'll be seeing a lot of him, Cooper. Byron essentially lives in the weight room. He was in the Olympics, if he hasn't told you already."

Cooper was visibly shocked. He remembered watching

the Olympics a few years ago but he hadn't seen anyone Byron's age.

Kelly read the confused look on his face and clarified. "Years ago, Cooper. Like fifty years ago."

"Oh," Cooper said.

"Going to get in again this year," Byron said and winked at him.

"He's been saying that for ten years."

"I should probably get back to work," Cooper said. "Make sure you put the weights back in order."

Byron laughed and looked at Kelly. "You heard him," Kelly said.

"Okay, okay!" Byron said, putting his hands up defensively.

Kelly turned to Cooper. "I need you to do me a favor. I need to leave early today, so I won't be able to teach my three o'clock aerobics class. I need you to—" Cooper was shaking his head, alarmed by where this was heading.

Kelly laughed. "I don't want you to teach the class, Cooper. Is that what you thought? Ms. Fisher is more than capable of leading them, but I want to track who shows up and who doesn't, so I want you to stand by the door with a clipboard and have them sign out as they leave. You okay with that?"

"Sure," Cooper said, enthusiastically, relieved that it was something well within his capabilities. "Is that what you wanted to talk to me about?"

"That's it," she said, and Cooper felt silly for getting so worked up about it.

"You're doing a good job, Cooper," Kelly said. "Keep it up and I'll give you more exciting responsibilities than cleaning bathrooms and mirrors."

She squeezed his arm before turning to leave and Cooper found himself blushing.

"Oh, no," Byron said, smiling at him. "I know that look!"

"What?" Cooper said.

"Don't 'what' me. Somebody has a crush on Kelly. Don't worry. Most men around here do at one time or another. I still do!"

"No I don't," Cooper said. "I mean, she's nice and everything."

"Yes she is, just as long as you don't get on her bad side. Nice looking, too—don't shake your head. You're old enough to notice."

"Maybe," Cooper said and he couldn't help grinning foolishly.

"Yeah, maybe. Too bad she's taken."

Cooper's smile died on his face.

"Maybe they're not getting along so well," Byron said, winking at him. "You never know."

Cooper wasn't sure what was happening. One minute he'd been gearing up to straighten things up, and the next he was having to admit to himself that Kelly was the reason he'd popped out of bed so easily this morning; that she was the reason he'd felt so relaxed and loose when he'd come in. She was the one he couldn't stop thinking about.

Cooper began picking up loose weights and putting them where they belonged, finding it hard to concentrate. As he worked, a few of the regulars said hello to him. A handful called him by name, which both surprised him and made him happy. Byron continued his workout. Cooper watched him through the reflection in the mirror. He had moved on to one of the machines. Cooper noticed that he was using almost the entire weight stack. Byron suddenly caught him looking and motioned him over.

When Cooper got there, Byron pointed towards the entrance and said, "That's your competition." Then he laughed. When Cooper saw who had walked in, he knew why it was so funny. The man was probably the largest human being Cooper had ever seen. Byron had muscles, but this guy was ridiculous.

"His real name is Chris, but everyone calls him The Green Giant," Byron said, and Cooper could see why. He was wearing green workout shorts and a green tank top. His hair reminded him of a peacock. It wasn't a Mohawk exactly. It was shaved all the way around the sides and back. The top was longer and was slicked back.

"That's Kelly's boyfriend?" Cooper asked, and he couldn't hide the disappointment on his face.

"Afraid so," Byron said, standing up and waving to The Green Giant. "I'll introduce you."

The Green Giant had a smile as big as his biceps. When Byron introduced him, The Green Giant grabbed Cooper's hand and said, "Nice to meet you, buddy!" Cooper's hand completely disappeared into his over-sized mitt. Now that he was up close, Chris looked like he could uproot trees and break through walls.

"Don't get too excited, he calls everyone that," Byron said.

The Green Giant patted Cooper on the shoulder and said, "So you're the one helping out around the place?"

"I clean the bathrooms," Cooper said. He wasn't sure why out of all his duties he had decided to share that one. "And other stuff," he added, but The Green Giant was already turning to leave. Kelly had poked her head out of her office and motioned him over.

Byron shook his head. "Big as a house and she has him gladly running in circles."

"He's huge," Cooper said.

The Green Giant had picked Kelly up and was twirling her around in circles. She complained, but she was beaming down at him.

"Muscles, Cooper," Byron said. "Women love muscles."

Cooper looked down at his skinny arms and legs.

"Yeah," Byron said, solemnly. "We've got a lot of work to do. How much do you weigh?"

"I have no idea."

"Well, let's go find out."

Byron led him over to one of the digital scales.

"Ninety-nine pounds."

"Is that good?" Cooper asked.

"No, that's not good. But the good news is you'll be able to put on weight quickly if you eat like him." Byron pointed to Chris, who had put Kelly down and was eating something out of a Tupperware bowl.

"Seven times a day he does that."

"Does what."

"Eats. And not junk, either. Chicken, rice, steak, vegetables, good stuff."

"You think I should eat seven times a day?"

"No, but at least five. You'll probably have a hard time convincing your grandfather to buy all that food, so this is what you eat: Tuna. Get lots of tuna. It's cheap and it's good protein. You like milk?"

"Yeah."

"Good. Drink a half gallon a day. Whole milk, not that low-fat, processed crap. Think you can handle that?"

"I think so."

"Do that and you'll be a giant like him before you know it."

Chapter Fourteen

Stanley usually went on the morning run to the grocery store, but he decided to wait for the six o'clock run so Cooper could go with him. Stanley didn't know why he wanted to go. All Cooper said when he asked him about it was that he wanted get a couple of things. He could have pushed him on it. After all, Stanley would more than likely be paying for whatever Cooper wanted to get, but he decided to let it go and wait and see. Stanley was just glad that Cooper was finally starting to relax and enjoy himself.

As they boarded the bus, Cooper seemed excited. Randy, the driver, did a double-take when he saw Cooper. Randy was in his twenties and probably not accustomed to seeing a young person getting on his bus. As Cooper walked by, Randy stopped him and told him that he'd let him drive on the way back. Cooper seemed relieved that Randy wasn't kicking him off and laughed, apparently at the thought of learning how to drive with a bus-load of old people.

Ned and Marie were sitting in the very back. Stanley and Cooper took the seats in front of them. Stanley couldn't quite hear what they were saying, but there was a fair amount of giggling. Every once in a while, Ned kicked the back of Stanley's seat, like they were suddenly back riding the school bus.

"He does that again," Stanley said to Cooper, "I think we should jump back there and rough him up."

As the bus pulled away from the curb, Ned leaned between Stanley and Cooper and said, "Four o'clock this morning I go to the bathroom like I always do and I see this huge—" Here Ned spread his hands apart to emphasize just how enormous it was—"shadowy form lurking just outside my window. I thought—"

"Was it Godzilla?" Cooper asked.

"Maybe it was a vampire," Stanley said, and Cooper and Marie laughed.

"Was he saying, 'Leeeeet meeee iiiiin!'?" Marie asked, scratching her nails down the window.

"Oh, for crying out loud," Ned said. "It wasn't a vampire and it wasn't Godzilla. It was that stupid horse, whatever his name is."

Stanley wasn't surprised. Over the last several days, he'd heard similar stories. Ms. Theron, for instance, had gone into the kitchen to get a cup of coffee and had returned to find *Ain't He Something* looking in her front window, apparently watching Days of Our Lives. She thought it was so funny that she removed the screen so he could fit his head through the window.

"Yeah, well," Ned said. "I don't know why we need a horse. We should have gotten a bird."

Ned settled back in his seat and Stanley and Cooper looked out the window. After riding in silence for a few minutes, Ned suddenly turned to Marie and said, "That's what your book needs!"

"What?" Marie asked.

"A bird! Every story needs a hero and a villain, right?" Ned said. "You have a cat, now you need a bird."

"But I like Francis. I don't want him going around

killing birds."

"No, no, the bird is the villain," Ned said. "That's why Francis is leaving home. The bird is making his life miserable."

"So now I've got a cat, an evil bird, and a three-legged dog. This is going to be some book!"

Stanley had to laugh. It was fun seeing Ned and Marie genuinely enjoying each other's company. Most women thought Ned was a clown, but Marie seemed to understand him in a way the others didn't.

Ned had apparently exhausted his creativity because he turned and leaned back in his seat and crossed his arms in front of him. Stanley turned back around. After a few minutes, Stanley was going to tell Cooper that this was the longest Ned had ever gone without talking when Ned poked Cooper in the shoulder and asked, "You still have my watch, right? Don't lose it. It's worth a fortune."

"Don't listen to him, Cooper," Stanley said. "I was with him when he got it. He won it at the State Fair a few years ago by throwing rings around bottles. I'm surprised it still works."

"Yes, but it was the grand prize," Ned reminded him.

"That reminds me," Stanley said, removing his Swiss Army watch and handing it to Cooper. "This is for you."

"Nice, Stanley," Ned said, laughing. "Giving your favorite grandson a broken watch."

Stanley ignored him, deciding not to tell him that Lillian had taken it to get a new battery the day before. She said she couldn't stand watching him walking around with a useless watch on his wrist.

"Really?" Cooper said. "I can have it?"

"Sure," Stanley said. "Now give Ned back his grand prize before he starts crying."

"Gives him a broken watch," Ned said. "Unbelievable."

The bus pulled up to the curb in front of the supermarket and they all piled out. When they entered the store, Marie and Ned went to the produce aisle and Stanley and Cooper headed for the lunch meat aisle. Cooper seemed to be trying to look every direction at once, but Stanley pretended not to notice. Stanley put a pound of ham in the basket and then they headed towards the toiletries so he could get paper towels. Halfway there, Stanley realized that he'd forgotten to get cheese. He was turning the cart around when Cooper said, "I'll go get it," and took the cart from him and disappeared around the corner.

When Cooper returned, Stanley saw that Cooper had gotten a whole lot more than just cheese. The entire bottom of the cart was lined with cans of tuna fish. On top of them were balanced three gallon containers of whole milk.

"Okay," Stanley said. "Did Ned put you up to this?"

Cooper shook his head. "This is what I need to eat to get bigger," Cooper said.

"Who told you that?"

"Byron," Cooper said, and it suddenly made sense. Working at the fitness center, Stanley knew it was only a matter of time before he ran into Byron.

"You like Byron?" Stanley asked.

"He seems nice. He's in good shape."

Stanley couldn't argue with that. Byron might be a showoff and hyper competitive, but he was in better shape than most men half his age.

"You want to look like Byron?" he asked.

"Everyone says I'm scrawny. Girls like muscles."

"They do?"

"Kelly likes muscles. Her boyfriend has the biggest muscles I've ever seen."

"You like Kelly?"

Cooper didn't answer. Stanley could tell he was on the verge of embarrassing him, so he backed off.

"You really need all this stuff?" Stanley asked. His immediate reaction was to put everything but two cans of tuna fish and one gallon of milk back where they came from, but, instead, he said, "Maybe we should get a few more cans of tuna while we're here."

Even though it was going to put a dent in his grocery budget, Stanley didn't really mind. In a weird way it seemed like Cooper was at a turning point. And if tuna and whole milk and muscles got him started down the right path, then he wasn't going to stand in his way.

"Holy half-a cow!" Ned said. He and Marie had pulled in behind them at the checkout counter. "You want some bread with that, Stanley?"

"It's not for me. Byron seems to think Cooper should build some muscles."

"Byron!" Ned said. "What's Byron know? He challenged me to a push-up contest, but I refused. I didn't want to embarrass him."

"Oh, please!" It was Marie who made the outburst, and she seemed as shocked as everyone else by her exasperation.

"I can do hundreds of them," Ned assured her.

"He can, Marie, just not all at the same time," Stanley said.

Ned turned to Cooper. "Are you going to eat vegetables or just forage around like a wild animal?"

"I'd hate to say it, but he's right," Stanley said. "We should probably go back and get some green beans or something."

"Good lord," Marie said. "Cooper, come with me. We'll go get some things while you two wait in line. We should probably get some apples, too. Don't want you getting scurvy."

"I can't eat apples," Ned said. "My teeth aren't strong enough."

"Well, then it's a good thing they're not for you," Marie said. "Come on, Cooper."

After they left, Ned looked at Stanley with a concerned look on his face. "Maybe I should get some oranges. I don't want to get scurvy, either."

****

When they got back to the facility, Cooper offered to take all the groceries to the room while Stanley and Ned went down to the activities room for a couple games of darts. Ever since Stanley had beaten him the last time at chess, Ned wanted to try his luck with other games.

It took less than an hour for Stanley to beat Ned six games to one. Ned begged for a chance to catch him, but Stanley refused, telling him, rightfully so, that they'd be there all night.

When Stanley returned to the room, he smelled the tuna even before he opened the door. Once inside, he found Cooper half sitting and half lying on the couch. There were four cans of tuna open on the coffee table in front of him next to a half-empty gallon of milk.

"You okay?" Stanley said.

Cooper blinked.

"Did you eat the tuna right out of the can?"

Cooper nodded.

"You know you're supposed to drain the water, right? Did you drain the water?"

Cooper shook his head.

"Did you drink the water? You didn't drink the water, did you?"

Cooper nodded.

"And then you drank all that milk?"

Cooper nodded.

"Oh, boy."

Stanley gathered up the tuna cans and returned the milk to the refrigerator. He was slightly appalled that all three gallons fit with no problem. Maybe Lillian had a point when she yelled at him about not stocking his refrigerator. He put the tuna cans in a grocery bag and tied it shut and put it in the trash. Then he opened all the windows and turned on the ceiling fan.

Returning to Cooper, he said, "You okay?"

Cooper shook his head.

"Can you speak?"

Cooper shook his head.

"Well, I guess try to sleep it off. Tomorrow I'll show you how to mix the tuna with mayonnaise—" Cooper suddenly stood up, covered his mouth with both hands and ran to the bathroom.

CHAPTER FIFTEEN

As if The Last Stop didn't already have enough in the way of animals, Harry decided he wanted to put in a koi pond on the strip of lawn just east of the main drive. What Harry envisioned was a large pond, ranging from one-foot to three-feet deep in the center, surrounded by flowers and a bench people could sit on. He was even thinking about adding a small beach area. He said it would be for the kids, but Cooper had a feeling it was just an excuse to put up the "No Swimming" sign that was gathering dust in Harry's maintenance shed.

Once Harry got an idea, he went to work on it immediately. The morning after Harry mentioned it, he'd already marked off the area and was getting ready to remove the grass. Cooper had some time before his shift started at the fitness center, so he decided to help.

The tuna debacle lingered fresh in his mind. He still felt slightly ill. He thought the digging might take his mind off of it. After an hour of digging by hand, though, Cooper was exhausted and suggested they get some sort of back hoe or something to make it easier.

"We could," Harry said, "but that would take all the fun out of it."

Even though it was hard, he enjoyed working beside Harry. He didn't know precisely when it had happened, but at some point he had decided that being busy was a good thing, even if it meant he was tired. The idea of lounging around all day, playing games on his phone like he used to, now seemed silly and somehow childish.

Later, when Cooper got to the fitness center to start his shift, the first person he ran into was Byron. He quickly, and with a little embarrassment, recounted his experience with the tuna and milk.

"You drank the tuna water! Guess you'll never do that again," Byron said. It didn't bother Cooper that Byron was laughing at him. He'd half expected it. "No harm in it," Byron continued. "You got excited is all. Unfortunately it doesn't work like that. Consistency and patience. I should have been clearer. Drink one glass of milk five times a day, and eat one can of tuna three times a day. Do that and you'll start putting on weight soon enough."

"Okay," Cooper said, relieved. He wasn't sure if he could do it, but he'd try.

"Now that we've got you eating, we need to get you moving," Byron said. "If you eat all that tuna and drink all that milk and don't do anything, you'll get bigger, all right, but not in a good way. So this is what you do: Every morning when you get up and every evening before you go to bed, I want you to do twenty-five push-ups and twenty-five sit-ups. Got it?"

"Like this?" Cooper said, dropping to the floor. He did two push-ups with his knees touching the floor.

"Cooper! Get up. Those are girl push-ups! You want Kelly to see you doing girl push-ups? Get down again, but this time, keep your back and legs straight. Flex your stomach muscles, now go down and come back up."

Cooper did. "That's a lot harder," he said when he was

done.

"You know why?" Byron said. "Because they're not girl push-ups. Let me see you do a sit-up."

Cooper did as he was told, but he had a hard time keeping his feet down. When he did them in gym class, he always had someone holding his feet.

"Stick your feet under a couch or something to keep them from coming up. I want twenty-five of each every morning and every night. You probably won't be able to do them all at the same time when you first start out, and that's fine. Just do what you can, rest, and then go again until you've done all twenty five. You'll build up to it. Once you can do it all in one set, we'll bump it up to thirty."

"Shouldn't I be lifting weights?"

"When you can handle your body weight, then we'll start worrying about adding weights," Byron said. Cooper had to admit that he was a little disappointed. He doubted that The Green Giant did push-ups and sit-ups.

And speaking of The Green Giant, he was spending most of his afternoons in the fitness center. Rumor had it that his regular gym was undergoing renovations so he was going to be using the fitness center for a couple of weeks. He was here again today, over by the dumbbell rack. Cooper tried not to stare at him, but it was hard. He was relieved to see that everyone else couldn't help staring at him, either. He marveled as The Green Giant approached the dumbbell rack and went right to the heaviest pair and began curling them with each arm.

"I want to do that," Cooper told Byron.

"Well, I hate to break it to you, but you can't do that right now. Once you build up some strength, we'll add some other things in—" Byron suddenly stopped and looked over Cooper's shoulder at someone who had just come in. The man looked a little older than Byron and he wore an outfit that seemed much too nice to workout in. The man got on one of the exercise bikes, looking over his shoulder and grinning at Byron.

"Stay here," Byron said. "I'll be back in a few minutes."

Byron stripped off his shirt and walked over and hopped on the bike next to the other man and they both started pedaling. They started out slow, but soon picked up the pace until both of them were pedaling furiously. They seemed to be going about the same speed until Byron stood up on the pedals and began really digging in. Byron was pedaling at such a furious pace that the bike started slowly inching forward. The other man laughed, shook his head, and settled back into a more reasonable pace. After another minute or so, Byron slowed and then stopped. He wiped the sweat off with his shirt and hopped off the bike.

"You're getting better, Aster," Byron told the man. "One day you'll give the ladies in the spinning class a real run for their money!"

Byron grinned at Cooper. "That'll teach him," Byron said, as he approached him.

"Teach him what?" Cooper asked.

Byron paused for a moment. "You know," he said, suddenly laughing, "I'm not real sure."

Both of them heard Kelly at the same time.

"You'd better get back to work," Byron said. "Kelly likes you, but that won't stop her from wringing your neck if she catches you messing around."

Cooper had been so busy with Byron that he hadn't noticed the weights strewn all over the place. He started gathering up the weight plates just in time for Kelly to walk in.

"You owe me one," Byron called to him.

"For what?" Kelly said.

"For saving his life," Byron said.

Kelly looked around and seemed to get what he meant.

"Cooper, come to the office when you're done," she said. "I have something for you."

Cooper quickly finished up. Byron was curious, too, and

helped him put all the weights back. When they were done, they went to Kelly's office. Byron hung around outside the door.

"Here," she said, sliding over a tub of something called Xtreme Muscle.

"What is this?" Cooper asked. There was a picture of a guy on the side with muscles almost as big as The Green Giant's.

"This will give you all the protein you need without having to eat all that tuna," she said.

Judging by the look on her face, she knew the whole story. Cooper wasn't surprised. If Stanley told Ned about it, the whole world probably knew by now. He didn't really mind. It was actually kind of funny.

Byron came into the office when he heard what they were talking about. "Don't give him that," he said. "He needs real food."

"He already eats real food," Kelly said. "No one should have to eat tuna three times a day."

"I'm teaching him the value of pain and suffering."

"How often do you eat tuna?" she asked him.

Byron looked at the ceiling and thought about it.

"Exactly," Kelly said.

"I paid my dues!" Byron said. "I used to eat it by the bucket-full. That and raw sardines. Popped them right down."

"Well, he's not training for the Olympics and now we know better." She turned to Cooper. "Drink that first thing in the morning and right before bed. That's what Chris does. He does three scoops, but you only need one." It took Cooper a minute to realize that she was talking about The Green Giant.

Byron snatched the tub off her desk and read the nutritional label. "Chris uses this?" he asked. "Let's see: twenty-five grams of protein, five grams BCAA's, five grams Glutamine . . . no sugar . . . Maybe I'll get myself a tub."

"What about real food?" Kelly said.

"Overrated," Byron said.

"But what about the raw sardines?" Kelly chided him.

Byron ignored her. "Chocolate Mint," he said. "I like Peppermint Patties."

"Thanks, Kelly," Cooper said, taking the tub away from Byron.

Just as he was turning to leave, Kelly stopped him. "I almost forgot. Amato dropped off your lunch." She tossed him a paper sack. "Sorry," she said. "But I'm pretty sure it's a tuna fish sandwich."

Chapter Sixteen

Cooper was up early. They had been hard at work on the koi pond for several days and it was just about done. The pond measured six-feet by twelve-feet and had a depth from one-foot at the shallow end to almost three-feet in the middle. Cooper thought that the digging would be the hardest part, but once the hole was dug, they had to put in a liner, and in order to hide the liner, they had to place large stones and rocks in strategic places and then fill in the cracks with gravel rock. Harry returned one morning with big slabs of slated rock that they used as shelves around the edges, giving the fish places to hide. Once that was done, they set up the filtration system and added moss and various aquatic plants. They were almost to the point where they were going to fill it with water and Cooper was excited.

Stanley was up early, too, and made enough scrambled eggs and toast for the both of them. Cooper wolfed them down, eager to get out the door. As he was running out, he remembered that he hadn't done his exercises yet. Even though he was tired and sore from moving all the rock and gravel the last few days, Cooper dropped down and started doing his push-ups. When he got to twelve, his previous best, they still felt easy, so he kept going. His arms started shaking at eighteen, but he still managed to get two more before his arms gave out.

"Was that twenty?" Cooper asked Stanley who'd been watching him, not quite believing that he'd gotten that much stronger that quickly.

"That's what I counted," Stanley said.

"Holy crow," Cooper said.

"Won't be long before you can do a hundred!" Stanley said.

"I bet I can do all twenty-five sit-ups," Cooper said.

"I'll bet you can," Stanley said, and Cooper dropped down and put his feet underneath the couch and started huffing and puffing his way to twenty-five. When he was done, he hopped up and headed towards the front door. Stanley stopped him. "You know, Cooper . . . It's really good what you're doing around here . . . I mean, working at the fitness center and helping Harry. You should be proud of yourself . . . Just thought you should know that."

Cooper hadn't stopped long enough to realize that what he had been doing was anything special, but now that he thought about it, he had been doing a lot lately. He'd been so caught up with everything that he hadn't given it much thought. It was just kind of what he did.

"No big deal," Cooper said.

"Actually, it is," Stanley said. "And this isn't just your grandfather talking. Everyone is noticing it."

Cooper had to admit that people had been treating him differently lately. Most of the regulars at the fitness center knew him by now, of course, but even residents that he'd never spoken to often smiled and said hello to him when they crossed paths.

"Thanks," Cooper said, opening the door and almost running over Ned. "Out of my way, buddy!" Cooper said, side-stepping Ned and jogging down the hall. He heard Ned ask Stanley, "What? Buddy? What is happening around here!"

When he was halfway to the barn, Cooper noticed Byron doing his morning calisthenics and he yelled, "Got twenty push-ups today!"

"Great! Now get thirty!" Byron yelled back.

When Cooper arrived at the barn to let *Ain't He Something* out of his stall so he could clean it, he found the horse tied to one of the railings and the stall already clean. He called Harry's name, and a moment later Harry appeared around the front of the barn.

"Morning!" Harry said. "Come see. Bring him with you." Harry led Cooper and *Ain't He Something* around the side of the barn and out to the fenced-off pasture.

"What do you think?" Harry asked. He'd put extensions on top of the fence all the way around the enclosure, so that now the fence was close to five feet tall. Most of the time it was okay if *Ain't He Something* roamed freely, but there were situations when it was better for all concerned if he was contained, and Harry didn't want him to have to spend those times in his stall.

"Think he'll stay?" Cooper said, leading *Ain't He Something* into the enclosure, letting him off the lead and closing the gate behind them.

"No way he's jumping—" Harry started, but before he could finish the sentence, *Ain't He Something* turned, galloped towards the fence and cleared it easily. When he was on the other side, he laid down on his side and rolled around in the grass. Cooper couldn't help but laugh.

"I guess he doesn't like fences," Harry said.

"Maybe he just likes the grass," Cooper suggested.

Harry looked around at the hard ground-cover in the fenced-off area and thought for a moment. "I've got an idea," he said.

They spent the next hour extending the fence so it included a patch of grass sufficiently large enough for *Ain't*

He Something to roll around on. When they were done, they once again led him in and let him loose. It took him a few minutes of exploring the new area before he came upon the grass section, but when he did, he immediately laid down. They'd been careful to do it in an area that was accessible to visitors. He might be okay with the new area, but not if it meant being denied the countless treats bestowed on him every day.

By the time they finished the fence, it was too late to fill the pond, so Harry promised they'd do it later that evening, and Cooper ran to the fitness center so he wouldn't be late.

Kelly met him at the door. She told him that she'd seen what he and Harry had been doing that morning and asked him if he wanted to take the day off.

"God no," Cooper said.

"That's what I thought you'd say," she said. "Oh, before I forget, Chris got you something, now that you're getting all buff and stuff."

Cooper followed her to the office and she threw him three green tank tops like the ones Chris wore. He didn't know what embarrassed him more: Kelly calling him buff, or the idea of dressing like Chris. The truth was that Cooper had been using Chris as a model of sorts, picking up some of his habits and mannerisms. He watched him workout. He watched how he greeted and interacted with people. But mostly he watched how he treated Kelly. He had to admit that he felt a pang of jealousy every time he picked her up and kissed her forehead, but Cooper could tell that there was no one Kelly would rather be with. Cooper thought he had been doing all this studying more or less incognito, but now it was obvious that Chris had known all along.

"Go put one of them on," Kelly said. "If you don't, it'll hurt his feelings."

Cooper did as he was told and returned to Kelly's office where he found Chris sitting in the chair opposite Kelly. When he saw Cooper, he sprung up and said, "Look at you!

You look just like me!"

"Not even close," Cooper said.

"Are you kidding? Look at those guns!" Chris enveloped one of Cooper's arms in one giant hand and squeezed.

"All right," Kelly said. "Now you're embarrassing him and he's got work to do. You don't have to wear the shirt if you don't want to, Cooper."

"No," Cooper said. "I kind of like it."

"I told you he'd like it," Chris said.

Later that afternoon when he was stocking the bathrooms, Cooper caught his reflection in one of the mirrors. He'd never liked the way he looked, so he never looked at himself if he could help it. He didn't particularly like looking at himself now, but he thought he should at least have some idea of where he was for later comparisons. He felt silly, but he took the tank top off and flexed his arm like he'd seen guys do in the magazines. It wasn't quite as bad as he'd expected, so he tried a few more poses. He was in the middle of a double bicep pose when the door opened and Kelly walked in.

"Might want to do that in the mens bathroom," she said.

"Sorry," Cooper said, scrambling to get his shirt back on.

"Don't be embarrassed," she said. "Chris does it all the time."

Chapter Seventeen

By the end of July, Cooper's routine was pretty well solidified. Byron had told him that it would take at least seven days to get used to the exercise routine, but it had taken him most of two weeks. Now, he did his push-ups and sit-ups without even thinking about it, and he was almost to the point where he could do fifty of each without stopping. Even Byron was impressed.

He didn't really notice the changes in his body until one morning when he noticed a vein popping out of his forearm while he was moving one of the dumbbells back to its proper place. That night, he took his shirt off and studied himself in the bathroom mirror. It was the first time he'd really looked at himself since Kelly caught him in the womens bathroom. Now that he did, he was surprised by what he found. His chest, once flat as a board, was starting to develop, and he was showing definition in the backs of his arms and shoulders. Even his stomach muscles were visible. He was so excited that he called for his grandfather, but when Stanley arrived, he was too embarrassed to show himself off.

He didn't know how much the protein shakes had to do

with his progress, but he now looked forward to drinking them, which hadn't always been the case. The first time he tried one, he put one scoop of the powder in a glass of tap water like the directions said and mixed it as best he could with a spoon, but it didn't mix well, and when he tried to drink it, large clumps of undissolved powder stuck in his throat, causing him to cough and spit the mixture all over the front of the refrigerator. Luckily his grandfather heard the commotion and came to the rescue. Without saying anything, he handed Cooper a roll of paper towels and dumped Cooper's concoction in the sink. Then he took the blender out from one of the bottom cupboards and plugged it in. He put a fresh scoop in the blender and added a cup of the whole milk and a banana and blended it until it was frothing. Then he poured it into a fresh glass and handed it to Cooper. "I can work wonders with the blender," Stanley said. "Just not the stove." Cooper drank it and was surprised by how good it tasted.

Even though the shakes replaced the canned tuna, Amato was still making him tuna fish sandwiches. Cooper finally got up the nerve to ask him if he could try one of the other sandwiches off the menu. Amato looked at him for a long, stern moment, and then asked, "What is this? You don't like my tuna?" Cooper quickly assured him that he liked it very much; it was just that some of the other items looked equally as good. Again Amato stared at him, squinting, apparently trying to see if Cooper was telling the truth. "The BLT looks good," Cooper told him, trying to end the awkwardness quickly, but Amato waggled his finger at him and said, "No, no. BLT! What is lettuce and tomato and bacon for a growing muscle man such as yourself? BLT! What you need is chicken! And let me tell you, I will make you a sandwich so full of chicken that . . . I will call it The Cooper! I'll get started on it immediately. Soon you will have muscles coming out of your forehead!"

Cooper wasn't a big fan of chicken, but Amato was so

excited about it that he didn't want to say anything. He liked the idea of a sandwich being named after him, though. He hadn't paid that much attention to the menu, but he was pretty sure he hadn't seen any items named after people. Amato was true to his word, showing up at the fitness center the next day holding a covered platter. He was smiling like Cooper had never seen before. It was such an odd scene that several of the residents stopped in the middle of their workout to see what was happening. Kelly stayed in the background with her hands on her hips, a bemused look on her face. Cooper tried to take the platter from him, but Amato held fast. "No! I must show you," he said, and ripped off the platter cover and revealed the largest chicken sandwich Cooper had ever seen. What looked like two whole battered chicken breasts were laid out over two halves of a hoagie roll. The whole thing was covered with some sort of sauce. Off to the side were sweet potato fries and two pickle spears.

"What do you think about that! You eat it with a fork!" Amato yelled, suddenly dropping the platter cover and producing a fork from out his apron pocket. "How many chicken sandwiches you know must be eaten with utensils?"

Cooper shook his head and frowned.

Amato said, "I can tell by your face that you've seen nothing like it. I would tell you how it is made, but there are too many eyeballs and earlobes here and it must remain a secret. The Cooper must remain a secret!" Then he handed him the platter and left, leaving Cooper to his meal and Kelly shaking her head and saying, "Unbelievable," under her breath.

The next time he saw Amato, Cooper told him that it would be okay with him if he made him The Cooper every day for the rest of his life. Amato pondered this for a minute before throwing his head back and laughing. "This is much, much too long. I will be long buried before that!"

Cooper continued looking after *Ain't He Something* in

the mornings before starting his shift at the fitness center. It didn't take long for the drawbacks of having a horse roaming freely to make themselves apparent. *Ain't He Something* didn't mind being in his pasture, but they could tell that he preferred being closer to the action, so they kept him out most days. Most horses tended to poop while they walked, and *Ain't He Something* was no exception, managing to drop it from one end of the property to the other. So much so that it was too much to handle on foot, so Harry taught Cooper how to drive the golf cart to make things easier. Now, every morning he loaded up the back of the golf cart with a shovel, a rake, a broom and heavy duty trash bags. Some of the residents started referring to him as the poop-catcher. While he was at it, Cooper took it upon himself to pick up any trash he saw lying around and emptied the various outdoor trashcans around the property. Harry, who prided himself on keeping the grounds clean of trash at all times, couldn't have been happier and said so. In the evenings, after his shift at the fitness center, Cooper would go down to the barn and lay out a fresh bed of hay. *Ain't He Something* usually wandered down about this time and Cooper spent a few minutes with him, getting him settled in for the night.

Ain't He Something's penchant for racing around the fitness loop continued. It took a while to realize that one of the things that set him off was the sound of Kelly's whistle. It didn't seem to matter where he was, if he heard the whistle, it was as if an imaginary starting bell went off and he'd rear up and take off running. Word spread quickly about the crazy horse running imaginary races and groups of people, residents and visitors alike, started hanging around the fitness loop, hoping to catch a glimpse. This happened so frequently that Harry put up custom signs warning people to keep alert, and he added a "Horse Crossing" sign to the main drive just for good measure.

Holy Moses and *Ain't He Something* had apparently come to some sort of agreement as far as giving each other space. They both preferred the courtyard, but both seemed to respect the other's need to have it to themselves. *Ain't He Something* spent most mornings there, but once the day warmed up, Holy would come out to lay under his favorite bush and *Ain't He Something* would amble off somewhere else. Lately he'd been taking more than a passing interest in the lobby itself, much to the surprise of those arriving or leaving. For Beverly's part, she thought it was hysterical to look up and see a horse staring at her through the glass at the very top of the double doors.

The lobby was the one place and Beverly was the one person that Holy wasn't interested in sharing. If he saw *Ain't He Something* headed that way, most times he'd cut him off and sit in front of the entrance until *Ain't He Something* snorted and went away. It was during one of these times that Cooper and Holy had what amounted to a bonding moment. Cooper had exited the lobby to find Holy watching *Ain't He Something* intently. So intently that he didn't immediately notice when Cooper knelt beside him and draped his arm around his back.

"Good boy?" Cooper said. Holy looked back at his hand and then directly at Cooper, but quickly turned his attention back to *Ain't He Something*. They stayed that way for a couple of minutes until *Ain't He Something* closed the distance, and then Holy stood up and barked. *Ain't He Something* stopped, snorted and shook his head, but he didn't retreat.

"Don't worry," Cooper told Holy. "I'll handle it," and redirected *Ain't He Something* back towards the barn. The next morning when he was emptying the trash in front of the lobby entrance, Beverly came out and said, "He likes you, you know." Cooper didn't know what she was talking about. "Him," she said, pointing to Holy Moses, who was staring at them out one of the lobby windows.

"He does?" Cooper asked.

"The minute he saw you, he started whining. He only

does that when he's excited to see someone."

Cooper couldn't really explain it, but out of all the experiences he had had so far, that was the one that made him the happiest. He knew it was silly, but he couldn't help it.

All this and more he told his mother on the phone. She'd checked in on him periodically, but she'd never had time to really talk. Now she did and Cooper was talking so fast that she had to ask him to repeat things. He told her about working for Amato and how he'd been fired. She sounded disappointed, but he quickly told her that Amato wasn't really that bad, and that he even brought him lunch most days. He told her about his new job at the fitness center and how he'd been helping Harry in the mornings. When he told her about *Ain't He Something*, his excitement must have carried all the way to California because she laughed and said she didn't know he liked horses.

"I didn't know I liked any of this!" he told her.

Then there was an abrupt silence. Cooper couldn't explain it, but he suddenly felt a strange tension coming from the other end of the line. He was about to say something when she said, ". . . I'm sorry, Cooper." She said it more to herself than to him. "I thought for sure you'd want to leave."

"What?"

"Here's the thing," she said, and Cooper knew what she was going to say before she said it and his heart sank. He'd been having trouble sleeping lately because he knew he was eventually going to have to leave. Now it seemed that eventually was going to be a whole lot sooner than he expected.

Chapter Eighteen

The morning after talking to his mother, Cooper woke up late. It wasn't surprising. He'd laid awake most of the night trying to figure out why the world was conspiring against him. His mom hadn't said why his school had moved up the registration date, but he was convinced they had done it to make his life miserable. He'd complained, even suggesting that she register for him, to which she responded, "For god's sake, Cooper, you have to get your picture taken for your student I.D card. I don't think they want a picture of your mother!" His last resort was his grandfather, who'd walked in to see what all the yelling was about. Stanley took the phone from him. He talked to her for a few minutes, but judging from the frown on Stanley's face, he wasn't getting anywhere, either. Stanley ended the conversation with, "Well, that's too bad. I wish there was some way he could stay," and Cooper knew he was sunk. Stanley tried to lessen the blow by reminding him that he would have been going home in a few weeks anyway, but the difference between two days and a few weeks seemed enormous. Cooper hadn't managed to give school a moment's thought the last two months, and now it sat at the forefront of his mind like a tumor, consuming all his thoughts. All the bad experiences dating clear back to elementary school came rushing back in a constant loop of misery.

Cooper suddenly didn't feel like doing his morning routine. What he wanted to do was stay in bed and hope that this latest development was just a bad dream, but he knew his grandfather wouldn't let him, and even if he did, Harry and Kelly would eventually come looking for him. He decided to blow off his exercises and his protein shake, though, figuring he could make it up later.

He knew Stanley wanted to talk to him, but he was already late. Besides, he didn't feel like talking, so he left while Stanley was in the bathroom.

Along with mucking *Ain't He Something*'s stall and going on poop patrol, he also took care of the fish. Before throwing a handful of fish food into the pond, he always skimmed the surface, removing any debris that had blown in. After that was done, he'd check the water level and clean up any trash visitors had left. This morning, the water level was several inches below where it should have been, so he decided to get the hose and top it off. While it was filling, Cooper saw Marie Chord coming out of the lobby with a cup of coffee in one hand and her writing pad in the other. She had taken to spending her mornings sitting on the little bench and watching the fish. Cooper liked her, of course, but Marie, more than anyone, had a way of getting him to talk, and he didn't feel like talking. He felt like being angry and it was hard to be angry around Marie, so he headed down towards the barn and tended to *Ain't He Something*'s stall. Normally when he was done, he'd hop in the golf cart and go on trash/poop patrol, but since he'd gotten a late start, it was almost time for his shift at the fitness center, so he decided to head up, picking up whatever he saw in route.

The idea of not working his last couple of shifts at the

fitness center never crossed his mind. The thought of disappointing Kelly was something he didn't like to entertain. Maybe it was just cleaning mirrors and bathrooms and straightening up, but it was his thing, just like taking care of *Ain't He Something* and going on trash patrol was his thing. The fact that he had skimped on the latter was probably the reason for the pit he was feeling in his stomach. If he didn't show up at the fitness center, Kelly would likely hunt him down. If he didn't pick up the trash and empty the trashcans and take care of the horse and the fish, Harry would probably just suck it up and do everything himself, which, somehow, was worse.

Kelly saw him as soon as he came in. She was showing one of the regulars a new exercise. They both said hello to him and then Kelly said, "Don't forget to stock the refrigerator with water, I plan on—" And then she stopped, probably because Cooper had suddenly turned a ghostly shade of white.

"Oh, my god," Cooper said.

"What's wrong?" she said.

"I forgot to turn off the water!"

The whole time he was running back to the pond, he was hoping that Marie or someone had noticed the water running and had turned it off. He just hoped that that someone wasn't Harry.

He could see it as soon as he rounded the corner. Not only was no one around, but the water was still running and the surrounding grass was its own miniature swampland. The fish, he noticed, with complete horror, had been carried out onto the grass and they weren't moving.

Cooper ignored the running water and hurried to get them back in the water.

The water suddenly shut off.

"No use," Harry said, rolling up the hose. "They're dead. We'd just have to scoop them out later."

Cooper put the fish down. He'd figured it was no use,

but it seemed wrong not to at least try to save them.

"Sorry," Cooper said. When he looked around, he noticed that the water had displaced all the flowers they had planted, too.

"Sorry," Cooper said again. He could feel Harry staring at him, but he couldn't bring himself to make eye contact.

"It happens," Harry said, but Cooper could tell by his tone of voice that it shouldn't have happened, and more than anything he wanted to be somewhere else, anywhere else.

"I'm supposed to be at the fitness center," Cooper said.

Harry nodded and Cooper headed back, feeling terrible.

When he got back, he restocked the water and cleaned the bathrooms like normal, but instead of cleaning the glass, he sat down on one of the exercise machines and stared out the window. He didn't know how long it had been, but it must have been a fairly long time because Kelly suddenly appeared, looking at him sideways. "Planning on doing any more work today?" she asked.

Cooper didn't say anything.

"You going to tell me what's going on or do I need to squeeze it out of you?" she asked.

Cooper turned away from her and didn't say anything.

"Well, I guess we're going to be here a while," she said, sitting down. "I'm not leaving until—"

"I killed the fish?" Cooper said.

"You did what?"

"The fish," Cooper said. "In the pond. I was adding water and I forgot to turn it off and now they're dead."

"That explains why you went running out of here, but that doesn't explain—"

"Harry's mad at me."

"I doubt it. You made a mistake."

"I know," Cooper said, "but I didn't have time to go around and pick up trash, so now he's doing it." Cooper pointed out the window at Harry, who was lapping the courtyard with a trash bucket.

"Well, that's easy to fix," Kelly said. "Get up."

"What?"

"Get up. Go out there and apologize and help him finish up."

"What? He's mad. He didn't say anything, but he didn't have to."

"Well, he's going to stay mad unless you go out there and apologize and make it right."

Cooper didn't want to, but he didn't really see how he had a choice. If he refused, she'd probably drag him out by his ear.

Cooper got a bag and a shovel out of the back of the golf cart and started on an area *Ain't He Something* had been frequenting lately. When the immediate area was clean, he returned everything to the golf cart and waited for Harry so they could go to the next spot. Harry returned a minute later and got in.

"Kelly okay with you being out here?" he asked.

"She kind of made me," Cooper said, and he saw a hint of a smile appear on Harry's face.

"Okay," he said. "When we're done, we'll get the pond back in order."

"Sorry," Cooper said. "I woke up late . . . I wasn't thinking. It was stupid."

And then Harry did the last thing in the world Cooper expected him to do: he started laughing. So much so that the whole golf cart shook.

"What's so funny?" Cooper asked.

"Jesus, Cooper. If you could have seen the look on my face when I saw those fish out on the lawn . . . It's bad. I shouldn't laugh, but that was a Kodak moment."

"Yeah, well," Cooper said. "You should have seen the look on my face when I remembered that the water was still running. Ask Kelly. She'll tell you all about it. That was a Kodak moment." Cooper had no idea what a Kodak moment was and Harry knew it, which made both of them laugh harder.

After a moment, Harry said, “You want to go with me to pick out more fish later?”

Cooper thought about it for a minute. Then he shook his head. “I think I’ve had enough fish for one day,” he said.

Harry smiled and nodded. “Not like you to wake up late,” he said. “You’re usually early. Everything okay?”

“Yeah,” Cooper said.

He wasn’t planning on telling anyone yet. There was part of him that thought, hoped, that if he didn’t say it out loud, it wouldn’t be true. Now he realized how silly that was.

“I’m going home tomorrow,” he said finally.

“I thought you were here until the end of the summer?”

“I have to register for school. They moved it up.”

“Well, that’s too bad. You’re going to be missed.”

“Now who’s going to help you?” Cooper asked.

“I’ll manage,” Harry said. “And that’s not what I meant.”

Chapter Nineteen

Cooper helped Harry for an hour before returning to the fitness center. Kelly saw him and raised her eyebrows questioningly. He nodded and smiled and she did the same. He got his cleaning supplies out of the closet and was about to start on the mirrors when he saw Byron. He was challenging a group of men to an arm wrestling match, but he wasn't getting any takers. When he saw Cooper, he said, "Get over here!" Cooper did, and Byron threw his arm around his shoulder and said, "Your education continues today! It's about time you start lifting weights. What do you want to work, shoulders? Chest? Legs? You tell me . . ."

Cooper looked around, but didn't say anything.

"Shoulders it is!" Byron said.

Cooper didn't know anyone who got so excited about lifting weights, but he had to admit that it was kind of contagious.

"You can show me, but there's not really any point . . . I'm going home tomorrow," Cooper said, feeling like this was just one more thing to pile on. He was finally at a point where he could start lifting actual weights and he had to go home.

Byron thought for a minute. Byron wasn't the type to get all mushy, but Cooper thought he'd get more sympathy than he did.

"So what you're telling me is that they don't have gyms in California?" Byron said. "They probably have one at your school, for crying out loud!"

Now that he thought about it, Cooper suddenly felt silly. He knew for an absolute fact that there was a weight room attached to the gym at his school, he just hadn't had a reason to notice it until now.

"Never mind," Byron said. "Today you get a crash course in weight training. Pretty soon you'll be the biggest kid in your class!"

Cooper liked the sound of that. He knew he'd never be the tallest kid in his class, but he had a feeling that if he was bigger and stronger than everyone else it would come with certain advantages, especially in high school.

"That sounds pretty good," Cooper said.

"Yeah it does. You should be paying me," Byron said. "I'm a former Olympian, remember?"

Even though Cooper knew that most of this was Byron's way of trying to make him feel better, he appreciated it.

"I need to do the mirrors and clean up before we start," Cooper said. "I'm way behind."

"Don't worry about the mirrors," Kelly said. She had an uncanny way of overhearing conversations at exactly the right moment. "If you promise to clean up after yourselves, I'll give you the rest of the day off."

Cooper frowned and stayed where he was.

"Well, what do you say?" Byron said.

Cooper looked around at all the weights scattered around and the mirrors all smudged up. "I'd like to get everything in order first," Cooper said. He couldn't explain it, but he didn't like the idea of not doing his job.

"Okay," Kelly said, "but don't say I never tried to do

anything nice for you."

"I want to do it tomorrow, too, before I leave," Cooper said.

"I'll make sure it's extra messy," Kelly said.

Cooper laughed and thanked her. Byron was shaking his head. "I wouldn't have believed it if I hadn't seen it with my own eyes and heard it with my own ears. What kind of fifteen-year-old boy volunteers to work when he doesn't have to? And you're not even getting paid!"

"A really good one," Kelly said and Cooper couldn't help blushing. Kelly noticed and quickly ruffled his hair and said, "Now if he'd just get a freaking haircut he'd be all set," and walked away.

Cooper turned to Byron. "It'll get done quicker if you help me," Cooper said, grinning at him.

"You might like working when you don't have to, but not me. In case you haven't noticed, I'm a frail old man," Byron said, laughing. "Find me when you're done."

"It might take me a while."

"I'll be here, unless that horse shows up. I tried to get on him this morning but he kept sidestepping me. I'll ride him if it's the last thing I do." Byron had expressed this desire before, but Cooper didn't think he was actually that serious about it until now.

"Have you ever ridden a horse?" Cooper asked.

"Nope. That's the beauty of it. If you never try things, you'll never know what you're missing . . . I should write that down some place."

"But he's a racehorse," Cooper reminded him. "What if he starts running?"

"All the better."

"You're not afraid of falling?"

"You get to be my age, you're not afraid of anything," Byron said. "Besides, it'd make one hell of a story."

Cooper agreed that it would.

While Cooper was cleaning up, it hit him just how much

he was going to miss this place. And it wasn't just the people he was going to miss. He couldn't put it into words, but he was going to miss the place itself. There was a feeling he got just being here. It was strange how things worked out. The feeling of anger and dread that he'd experienced when his mother told him that he was going to spend his whole summer at an old folks' home was now the exact same feelings he was experiencing about the idea of leaving. He felt bad about thinking of it as an old folks' home. It might be technically accurate, but Cooper didn't think of any of the people he'd met as being old. Not even his grandfather, and grandfathers were supposed to be old.

It took Cooper the better part of an hour to finish straightening up to his liking. When he was done, Byron gave him a tour of all the equipment and how to use it. There was so much that at one point Byron told him to go to the office and get a pen and paper, which he did. Byron showed him exercises for his arms and his shoulders and his back. He showed him half a dozen movements with dumbbells and half a dozen more with barbells. Then he moved on to the various machines. When The Green Giant saw what they were doing, he joined in, giving him tips and alternative movements, so much so, that when it was over, Cooper was exhausted and he hadn't even done anything.

"Before you leave," Byron said. "Chris and I will write you up a four day a week program that'll get you started. Do that for three or four months and you'll figure everything else out. You'll have to figure out how much weight to use on your own. Just remember that you want the weight heavy, but not to the point where you start cheating and using all sorts of muscles that aren't supposed to be involved. But make sure it's challenging. Doing ten repetitions with a weight you can do for twenty repetitions is a waste of time."

"What if my school doesn't have the equipment?" Cooper asked.

"They should at least have free-weights. If they don't,

shame on them. When in doubt, do your push-ups and sit-ups and add in bodyweight squats and pull-ups. If they don't have a pull-up bar, find a tree branch. Back when I started, guys curled buckets full of water and lifted logs over their heads . . . Now that I think about it, maybe you should see if your mom will buy you a weight set you can put in the garage."

"Maybe," Cooper said. He liked the idea. That way he could workout whenever he wanted. He didn't know if his mother would buy him one or not, but it wouldn't hurt to ask.

"Now promise me," Byron said. "You have to keep this up. I won't be there to whip you back into shape if you slack off. You might not love it now, but in time you will. Eventually, you'll be like me—"

"No he won't." Kelly had sneaked up on them again. "You are one of a kind."

Byron laughed.

"You might end up like Chris, though," Kelly said, and Cooper suddenly knew what haircut he was going to get.

Chapter Twenty

Later that evening, Cooper, Stanley, Ned, Lillian and Marie went to dinner together. Stanley thought it would be nice for the five of them to have some time before Cooper left. Cooper's mother would be there in the morning and Cooper planned on doing his regular morning duties, so there wasn't going to be an opportunity for all of them to get together. Cooper had also said something about wanting to get a haircut before he left, which was totally unexpected. He felt bad about Cooper's time being cut short, but the changes he had seen in Cooper in such a short time made him proud beyond measure. Stanley knew that Cooper wasn't looking forward to returning to his old life, but he felt confident that he was better equipped to handle it.

Cooper and Stanley arrived at the restaurant early and got the booth in the corner. The other three hadn't arrived yet. Cooper hadn't said much on the walk down, and he didn't say much now that they were seated, either.

"You all right?" Stanley asked.

"Yeah," Cooper said and sighed. "I mean, not really. I don't want to go. But I'm okay, I guess."

"You worried about going back to school?"

"Of course he is!" Ned said, scooting into the booth opposite them. Marie followed. "Nobody likes school," Ned said. "Couldn't stand it myself. This teacher I had used to rap my knuckles all the time with a ruler—"

"Let me guess," Stanley said, "because you talked too much?"

"I'm a nervous talker, what can I say? You should have seen me when the Barkley triplets used to take turns smacking me in the back of the head. I kept trying to tell them stories."

They could hear Lillian before they saw her, which wasn't surprising. When she got to the table and slid into the booth next to Cooper, she patted his knee and said, "Don't believe a word Ned says. His memory is as short as he is."

Marie laughed. Ned looked at her sideways. "Really?" he said.

"What?" Marie said. "It was funny."

"You're just lucky Cooper is leaving us," Lillian said. "If he was here much longer, he'd dwarf you in no time."

"Please," Ned said.

"Look at the bright side," Lillian said, turning to Cooper. "You don't have to spend weeks dreading going home. This way it's like ripping off a bandage."

"Which hurts, by the way," Stanley said.

"Yes, but it's done and over with. Worst thing in the world to be sitting around stewing about things."

"I guess," Cooper said.

"So what do you want to do when you're out of school?" Marie asked him.

"What do you mean?" Cooper asked.

"When you're done with school," Marie said. "Do you want to go to college or get a job or what?"

"Maybe you want to be a writer like Marie?" Ned said. "She's written almost fifty pages."

Marie rolled her eyes. "Only a hundred and fifty to go,"

she said.

"That's pretty long for a kids book," Cooper said.

Marie was about to take a drink of water but stopped and set her glass down and looked at him cockeyed.

"Kids book?" She said it more to herself than to Cooper. Then she smiled. "Of course!" she said. "Here I am trying to write the Great American Novel and I have a cat as a main character, plus a three-legged dog, for god's sake. Cooper, you are brilliant!"

Ned frowned and bobbed his head from side to side. "Good one, Coop," Ned said. "I probably would have thought of it eventually."

Tracey came by to tell them that their food would be out in a minute or two. When she was gone, Lillian turned to Cooper. "You might be brilliant, but you still haven't answered the question."

"I don't know. I've never thought about it that much," Cooper said.

"Might be a good idea to start," Lillian said. "It'll help you get through school. Things are easier when you have a good reason for doing them."

"That's deep stuff," Ned said.

Marie smacked him on the knee.

"What?" Ned said. "I was being serious."

Lillian ignored him and said to Cooper, "You like that silly horse, don't you?"

"Yeah."

"Well, maybe you want to work with animals."

"You can do that?" Cooper said. "I mean, with horses?"

"Sure," Stanley said. "You can even work at the racetrack if you want. California has a couple of the best in the country."

"Oh, how I miss Del Mar," Ned said.

"You've never been to Del Mar," Stanley said. "Anyway, there's Santa Anita, too."

"What would I do, though?" Cooper said. "I don't think

I want to ride them."

"You're getting too big anyway," Stanley said. "You have to be really little to be a jockey."

"Ned could be a jockey," Lillian said. "Not you."

They all laughed, even Ned.

"There's all sorts of things you can do," Stanley said. "I think there's even a school you can go to."

"If you don't want to work at the track itself, you could be a trainer," Ned offered.

"Train horses?"

"Sure," Ned said. "You think they're born knowing how to race?"

"I don't think Mom would like that very much."

"Well, maybe you could be a veterinarian," Marie said.

"You'd better learn to love school," Lillian said.

"I don't think I'd be very good. I can't even take care of fish."

No one but Stanley knew the story, so Cooper spent the next few minutes giving them the highlights. When he was done, Ned said, "Jesus, kid. I didn't know you had it in you," and Marie kicked herself for deciding to take a walk that morning instead of sitting by the pond like she usually did.

"Please," Lillian said. "You know how many fish die in fish tanks every day? You know the fish in the lobby, Cooper? Well those aren't the first ones. Beverly didn't feed the first ones and they ended up eating each other."

"Seriously? Why didn't she feed them?" Cooper said.

"Call it an oversight," Lillian said. "Ask her about it."

"Better not," Stanley said. "She's still sensitive about it. The point is that everyone makes mistakes. The fact is that you're at an age where you can do anything you want, but you have to make a decision, otherwise—"

"You end up a drug-head," Ned said.

"Oh, Ned," Marie said. "Cooper would never do drugs."

Stanley thought back to Ned's theory that Cooper was smoking marijuana and he smiled to himself. Stanley could tell Cooper was getting overwhelmed by the topic of conversation, so he decided to change the subject. "In the meantime," he said. "You can help out around here. I'll bet they'd even pay you next time."

"What do you mean?"

"If you wanted to spend your vacations out here, I'm sure it would be fine," he said. "You could spend Christmas break, spring break and summer, too, if you wanted."

"Slow down, sport. Let's not go crazy," Lillian said, squeezing Cooper's hand. "We don't like him that much."

"I can really come back?" Cooper asked.

"You'll have to clear it with your mother," Stanley said, "but I'll put in a good word for you."

"So there you go," Ned said. "Quit being so gloomy. Three or four months of school and then you can come back and hang out with old people again."

"That's not so bad," Cooper said.

"By that time, maybe I'll have my book done . . . My kids book done," Marie said.

Tracey brought them their food and they spent the next fifteen minutes eating and talking about things other than what Cooper was going to do with his life. Stanley could tell that Cooper was relieved. When they were getting up to leave, Ned put a hand on Stanley's shoulder and asked, "So, have you told him yet?"

"Told me what?" Cooper said.

"Eva gave me some money to give you so you can replace your skateboard."

"Eva?"

"The woman who almost ran you over in the parking lot," Ned said. "Just think, now you can skate naked!"

Cooper turned to Stanley. "Do I have to use it for a skateboard?"

"You can use it for anything you want," Stanley said. "It's your money. You don't want a skateboard anymore?"

"How are you going to skate naked without a

skateboard?" Ned asked.

"Oh, stop it, Ned!" Marie said.

"I do want a skateboard, but I think I'd like a weight set more," Cooper said.

The four of them collectively raised their eyebrows and nodded.

"Gonna be a lady-killer," Lillian told him and Marie agreed.

They made their way to the exit, but before they got there, they heard the unmistakable voice of Amato as he stormed out of the kitchen and made his way towards them. "What is this I hear you are leaving? You were going to leave and not say goodbye to your dear friend, Amato? Who will sweep my floors so good?"

"He doesn't sweep anymore," Ned said.

"You think I don't know this? The memory of the young riff raff forever doing circles going Broom! Broom! is near to my heart."

Cooper surprised himself and everyone else when he asked Amato if he needed help washing the dishes before he left. Amato waggled is finger at him, thought for a moment, then burst into violent laughter. "Look how far he has come! He makes jokes! This is why I make a chicken sandwich in his honor."

"He might be coming back for Christmas break," Stanley told him.

"And next summer," Cooper added.

"What is this? Fantastic! We will have our very own little riff raff . . ." Amato patted his shoulder. "Not so little anymore. Going to be very large muscle man. Pretty soon he will have muscular earlobes!"

Cooper was going to thank him for everything and tell him goodbye, but Amato was already headed back to the kitchen, yelling at Nathan to make a fresh batch of tater tots.

Chapter Twenty-One

On Cooper's last day, Stanley accompanied him to get his haircut. They were going to have to be fast. By the time Cooper was done with his morning duties and had gotten the fitness center in order, it was almost nine-thirty. Cooper's mother was going to be there at ten, and she was likely going to be in a hurry.

Stanley had been getting his haircut by Frank the barber since he took over for a man named Ed almost five years ago. Unlike Ed, who was perfectly happy using a dining chair as a barber chair, and couldn't really do much more than trim up the hairstyle you came in with, Frank was a true barber. The shop was in a little room between the activities room and the movie theater. It hadn't really looked like a barbershop from the outside until someone donated a little light in the shape of a barber pole and Harry hung it outside the door. And unlike Ed, Frank insisted that he have a proper barber chair, as well as a variety of sharp scissors, high quality clippers, several different styles of picks and combs, and a good handheld mirror, all of which was provided.

While Stanley didn't go quite as often as he should,

others went nearly every week, whether they needed a trim or not, just to sit and chat in the little waiting area chairs and watch Frank work.

Frank was a seasoned barber and stayed up on most of the current styles, but when Stanley and Cooper arrived and Cooper told Frank what style he wanted, Frank was visibly taken aback and made Cooper repeat his request several more times.

"Let me get this straight," Frank said. "You want me to shave it all the way around," and here he made a dramatic sweeping circle with his hand. "But you want me to leave the top the way it is?"

"Yes," Cooper said.

"You don't just want a buzz cut?" Frank asked. "It'll keep you cool in the summer."

"Nope," Cooper said.

Frank looked to Stanley for help. Stanley shrugged.

"And what do you want me to do with all of this," Frank said, running his hand through the top of Cooper's hair, which had grown unchecked for months and was five or six inches long.

"Leave it," Cooper said.

Frank shook his head. "I don't think I can do this," he said. He turned to Stanley and said, "And you're okay with this?"

"It's not my hair," Stanley said. "It seems pretty straight forward. If you can't—"

"Of course I can do it!" Frank snapped. "I just don't know if I want to. He has such nice hair." Frank turned back to Cooper. "Maybe you could get me a picture or something so I understand exactly what you want."

"I'll do you one better," Cooper said and hopped out of the chair and raced out of the shop. He returned a few minutes later with The Green Giant in tow. Stanley had seen Chris often enough, but he was always slightly shocked when he saw him up close. Frank was obviously seeing

Chris for the first time and was nearly speechless, especially because Chris's hair was precisely the style Cooper was asking for. Stanley had been wondering what it was about this particular hairstyle that had such appeal, now he thought he understood. Between the haircut, the matching tank tops, and his new interest in weight training, it was obvious that Chris had made a big impact on Cooper.

"Okay, okay," Frank said, sitting Chris down in the chair and spinning him around a couple of times. "I see what you mean . . . I don't know. He can get away with it, but you . . . You're sure about this?"

Cooper assured him that he was. Chris got out of the chair and patted Cooper on the head. Then he turned to Frank and patted him on the head, too, and said, "Make it look good, doc," which Frank must have found confusing and terrifying all at the same time.

By the time Frank had Cooper seated and ready, a small crowd had formed in the waiting area. Stanley knew that Ned was going to show up and maybe Lillian, but Marie had come along, too, and between all of them they'd brought a crowd of onlookers, all apparently wondering what was so interesting at the barbershop. Those who couldn't squeeze into the waiting area peered in through the windows. When Cooper saw everyone, he was visibly embarrassed. Frank remarked that it was the craziest thing he'd ever seen.

"They all with you?" Frank asked Cooper.

"I don't know," he said. "I guess so."

"Okay," Frank said, spinning him around one final time before grabbing the clippers. He studied them for a minute and concluded that they needed to be oiled. Stanley thought he was just stalling.

"Get on with it already!" Ned yelled.

"Okay, okay," Frank said, turning on the clippers and shaking his head. "Here we go." He said it like he was about to jump out of an airplane.

But before Frank could start, Kelly suddenly elbowed

her way through the crowd and told him to wait. She turned to Chris and shoved him hard. "Did he put you up to this?" she asked Cooper.

Cooper shook his head.

"It's enough that you wear the tank top. You don't have to turn into his clone."

"He swears this craziness is what he wants," Frank assured her. Stanley cringed, noticing that Chris was still within hearing distance, but if he was bothered by the comment, he didn't show it.

"Well, I hope you weren't planning on blending in at school," Kelly said, and for the first time Cooper frowned.

"No," he said after a moment. "I don't think I want to blend in this year."

Once that was settled, Frank took a deep breath, set the clippers on high and got to work, wincing at all the hair falling to the ground. It didn't take long. After a few minutes, Frank spun him around in the chair so he could see himself in the mirror.

"Remember," Frank said, "this is what you wanted." Frank watched Cooper and waited for a reaction. It wasn't exactly like Chris's, but it was pretty close. Frank watched as Cooper ran his hand through the top, which was still long and flopped over to one side.

"Does it look silly?" Cooper asked.

"Here," Frank said, "let's at least put something in it to hold it in place."

Stanley was relieved to see that the styling gel made a huge difference. He didn't like it, of course, but it was definitely better.

"Now that's a haircut!" Chris said. Cooper got out of the chair and Kelly came over to get a better look.

"Let's get a look at you," she said, and a strange look came over her face.

"Does it look stupid," Cooper asked her.

Kelly cocked her head sideways, smiled and said,

"You're going to have to beat all those high school girls off with a stick."

"Why would he do that?" Chris asked and Kelly punched him in the arm.

"See how she treats her future husband?" Chris said.

"Husband?" Cooper asked. Kelly held out her hand to show him her ring. Even from Stanley's vantage point he could see that it wasn't a standard engagement ring. It was much too large for one, and the color was all wrong.

Cooper frowned and looked up at her. "Is it supposed to be green?" he asked.

Kelly smiled at Chris. "Of course it is," she said.

****

The haircut had taken longer than expected. By the time he'd said goodbye to everyone at the barbershop, it was almost ten o'clock and he hadn't even packed yet. He knew his mom would be in a hurry when she got there, and he still wanted some time to say goodbye to Holy Moses and Beverly. Luckily, they were usually in the same spot. Stanley told him that he'd gather up his things and meet him out front, giving Cooper a few minutes before his mom arrived.

On his way to the lobby, Cooper stopped by the restaurant and asked Amato if he could have some cheese to give to Holy Moses before he left.

"Give him this," Amato said, getting a chunk out of the refrigerator. "That monster loves extra sharp cheddar."

Cooper again tried to tell him goodbye, but Amato waved him off. "You'll be back," he said. "We are irresistible."

Cooper thanked him for the cheese and ran to the lobby.

Beverly was visibly startled when she saw him and his new haircut and it made him laugh. He couldn't wait to see the look on his mother's face when she saw him. He was wearing one of the green tank tops, too. Holy Moses, he was glad to see, was lying beside Beverly's chair, and even he seemed to do a double-take. He'd been snoring when Cooper first came in, but once he got a whiff of the cheese, his ears perked up and he opened his eyes and sniffed the air.

"Well, come here!" Cooper said, and Holy gave him a look suggesting that perhaps it would be better if Cooper came to him.

"Get up, you big lug," Beverly told him.

Holy complied and padded over to Cooper and sat down.

"I hear you're leaving us," Beverly said.

"Yeah, my mom will be here any minute."

"Well, it was real nice having you around," she said. "Now who's going to help me keep all these oldsters in line?"

Cooper laughed. Holy whined and jabbed an enormous paw into Cooper's leg.

"I'm coming back during Christmas break," Cooper told her.

"Glad to hear it," Beverly said. "You better give that to him. He likes you, but that doesn't mean much when it comes to cheese."

Just at that moment, Cooper heard a slightly familiar voice, though he couldn't immediately place it. Then he heard, "Marcus! Get over here! We don't have time for this!" and he knew exactly who it was. Beverly rolled her eyes up at the ceiling and put a hand over her face.

Marcus ran in with his mother following behind him, looking exhausted. Marcus saw Cooper, but if he recognized him from their encounter a couple months previous, he didn't show it. Then he saw Holy Moses.

"Let me give it to him!" he yelled, running over and taking the cheese from Cooper. Cooper's initial reaction was anger, but he caught Beverly smiling at him and shaking her head.

Holy turned his attention to Marcus.

Marcus held the piece just out of Holy's reach. "You want it boy? You want it?"

Holy tried to take the cheese, but Marcus pulled it back and roared with laughter.

"Marcus! Knock it off!" his mother said. "We don't have time for this!"

Again, Marcus held the cheese out and started yelling out commands, "Sit down! Lay down! Play dead dog!" Holy whined, which signaled frustration. Cooper had never seen Holy show such restraint. He knew it wouldn't last. Cooper started to tell Marcus that he'd better give him the cheese or he'd be sorry, but Beverly stopped him with a wave of her hand and said, "No, no, Cooper. Let Holy have his fun."

Cooper realized what she meant and was settling in for the show, when he heard a car horn. He knew who it was, but he ran over to the window and looked out just to be sure. His mother was parked just outside the front entrance, leaning over the passenger seat so she could see out the other window. Cooper looked at Holy Moses and then at Beverly.

"I'll fill you in on what happens the next time you're here," Beverly said.

Cooper laughed and pushed through the double doors. As the doors were closing, he heard Marcus's laughter turn to shrieks, followed by a thud that could only mean one thing.

"There he is," Stanley said. He was putting Cooper's things in the trunk.

"Holy crow," Cooper's mom said. "Look at you!"

Stanley shut the trunk and came around and put a hand on Cooper's shoulder. "All set," he said.

"What in the world have you done to my son, daddy?" she asked.

"Not a thing," Stanley said. "He did it all on his own." Then he turned to Cooper. "You need anything you let me know, okay?"

Cooper said he would.

"And take care of that watch," Stanley added. "I don't think they make them like that anymore."

Cooper said he would and gave Stanley an awkward hug.

"All right, all right," Stanley said. "Get out of here while you still can."

As they drove by the pond, Cooper saw Harry. He had the hose out and was topping off the water level. Cooper rolled down his window and told his mom to stop the car.

"Don't forget to turn the water off!" Cooper yelled.

Harry turned and laughed. "So you're out of here, huh?"

"Yeah, I'll be back, though," Cooper said, turning to his mother, who'd raised her eyebrows and laughed.

"Good. Thinking about putting in an outdoor pool next summer," Harry said. "Could probably use some help."

"Sure," Cooper said.

"This time we'll get something to help with the digging."

"Nah, that would take all the fun out of it," Cooper said and waved as they pulled away.

After a moment, Cooper's mom looked at him and said, "You really like this place, don't you?"

Cooper thought about it. "Yeah, I really—" Cooper started, but his mom had suddenly stopped the car and was leaning her head out the window.

"What?" Cooper said.

"There's some crazy person back there riding a horse!"

THE END

THANKS FOR READING!

Have You Read the First Two Books?

Praise for THE LAST STOP

--The most important gauge for me was that I actually laughed out loud . . . This is a thoroughly entertaining and lovely book.--

--I hope when I hit that age that I live somewhere just as ludicrous and full of such lively characters. Holy Moses.....need I say more!!!!!--

Praise for GRANDMA VS. THE TORNADO AND OTHER STORIES

--There is no way you can read this book and not either chuckle or laugh out loud! Once you start reading, it's as if all your burdens somehow fall off your shoulders.—-

--Great, loved it, laughed throughout the book.—-

If You Enjoyed Cooper's Last Resort, Please Consider Leaving a Quick Review.

For the latest news, join The Last Stop Bulletin Newsletter here: http://eepurl.com/buXIOz

kirtboyd@netscape.net

Printed in Great Britain
by Amazon